Pretty is as Pretty Dies

A Myrtle Clover Cozy Mystery, Volume 1

Elizabeth Spann Craig

Published by Elizabeth Spann Craig, 2010.

PRETTY IS AS PRETTY DIES

First edition. September 28, 2010.

Written by Elizabeth Spann Craig.

In memory of Amma, Mary Ligon Spann.

Prologue

Parke Stockard wouldn't have ended up popped-over-the-head dead if she hadn't been bent on making mischief that morning. To be fair, though, she couldn't have known she'd messed with the wrong person this time—one who solved their Parke Stockard plight by leaving her dead at the church altar.

Waking up in her pink satin sheets that morning, she'd mulled over some malevolence. While brushing her hair model-quality blonde hair, she'd concocted even more nastiness. And, when driving her Champaign-colored BMW convertible to church, she made the fateful phone call that started the day on its slippery slope.

If Parke had—for once—rejected her baser instincts, she'd still be happily dreaming up devilment this very day. If she'd only listened to the *good* Parke buried deep in the nether regions of her murky conscience. Or had second thoughts and remembered she was on her way to *church*. But she didn't and the stage was set for murder in the sanctuary.

Early-morning summer light peeked through stained glass windows, its gentle light illuminating the flower arrangement on the altar. The withering glare Parke leveled at it should have vaporized the intrepid bouquet on the spot. Unscathed by her fury, the black-eyed Susans and daisies sassily defied her.

Parke vowed to do something about Kitty. Scavenging the roadsides for the altar arrangements was not going to work. Good Lord, next she'd be sticking Queen Anne's lace in Mason jars with chickweed filler. Dumping the weedy bouquet in a trash bag, Parke pulled out roses from her canvas tote and rapidly positioned them in a heavy crystal vase.

Intent on fixing the immediate crisis of the unsuitable arrangement and the long-term problem of the locals' ignorance, Parke didn't notice the sanctuary doors open. A harsh voice caught her attention.

"You!" Parke said scornfully. And then she picked the last fight of her life—thirty minutes later, pretty Parke Stockard was dead...

Chapter One

Several days earlier:

It was a warm, but not yet muggy, 7:00 a.m. on what would become a blistering summer day. Sensible, elderly citizens of Bradley, North Carolina, were contentedly puttering about before the heat took a turn into truly oppressive territory. They plucked tomatoes off their backyard vines for lunch, refilled feeders for cardinals and bluebirds, wrestled with the complexities of the daily crossword, or munched leisurely bowls of Grape Nuts under humming screened-porch fans. Myrtle Clover could not be included among this placid part of the populace. An early-morning phone call had fired her up into a froth. Parke Stockard.

An unwelcome glimpse of herself in a shiny, copper kitchen pot revealed an Einstein-like image scowling back at her. She patted down her wispy poof of hair into a semblance of order and squinted at the rooster clock hanging on her kitchen wall. No, it wasn't too early to call Elaine. Myrtle's toddler grandson functioned admirably as Elaine's alarm clock. What did it matter that he preferred watching the *Teletubbies* at 5:30 a.m.? In his baby head, everyone *should* be eager to watch Laa-laa wrangle her big, yellow ball from Dipsy's clutches.

Elaine answered the phone with a weary hello. The early mornings must be hitting her pretty hard. Her voice was gravelly like she'd swallowed half of Jack's sandbox.

"Parke Stockard is bad news, Elaine. Bad news. The whole town is riled up about her. And let me tell you what she's done to *me*."

Elaine was, really, trying to listen to her mother-in-law. Ordinarily, multi-tasking was her forte. But, with the cordless phone crunched between her ear and her shoulder as she cleaned up Cheerios her son had cheerfully tossed onto the linoleum, she couldn't fully focus on the phone call. "Um. Really?" Elaine stretched to reach the crumbs on the other side of the chair and felt much older than thirty-six.

Myrtle paused for effect. This effect would have been more imposing if Elaine had been able to see Myrtle draw her octogenarian but sturdy frame to its full six feet. "She just finagled more space for her *Bradley Bugle* column."

Elaine pulled the pepper shaker out of Jack's chubby two-year old fist, prompting a howl of protest. She winced at the noise. "Why is that a problem for you?"

"Because now my helpful hints column is being cut by half! Sloan Jones, the editor, called me this morning first thing to let me know. Coward. Probably hoping I'd still be snoozing in bed and he'd get my answering machine. This town needs my helpful hints a lot more than the crud Parke Stockard spews on paper. That pointless 'Posing Prettily with Parke' column. Wretched woman." She paused as Jack's howling reached her ears. "Are you besieged? Is Jack making that racket? What *are* you doing to my darling grandson?"

Elaine jogged towards the back of the house, the darling grandson in hot pursuit. Taking refuge in the master bedroom, she yanked the door shut, locking it quickly. She brushed her black bob out of her eyes with a yellow latex-gloved hand. Elaine hoped Jack, now flinging his small body angrily against the door, would soon discover that the *Teletubbies* perma-played on the den TV. Looking down, she discovered she still clutched the pepper shaker. She set it down on a dresser and plucked off the latex gloves. "Nothing. He...it's time for his nap as soon as I get off the phone with you. He got up at 4:30 for some reason today and so it's already naptime." She cut off her own hysterical laugh. Elaine was a morning person, but in no way interpreted 4:30 as qualifying as morning.

"Uh....," Elaine rounded up her scattered thoughts. "I think her column is called 'Lovely Living with Parke', Myrtle. Why would Sloan cut your articles? Everyone raves about them."

Myrtle plopped down at her living room desk and opened a computer file, glaring at the copy. "So my column has been kind of wacky the last couple of weeks. But you wouldn't believe the tips people mailed in to me. I made do with that tip about Ivory soap under fitted sheets relieving leg cramps." Myrtle snorted.

"And the tip about stopping nosebleeds," Elaine helpfully reminded Myrtle. She noticed with relief that the screaming had trailed off and prayed his little feet were plodding off to the den.

"Oh right. That old wives' tale about dropping a set of cold keys down the neck of the afflicted." Myrtle morosely read the offending article off the computer screen.

"Sloan thinks I'm dabbling in the occult. But they weren't *my* tips, after all."

Elaine cautiously opened the bedroom door and peeked down the hall. No demented toddlers lurking there, only their sullen, teenaged French exchange student, stumbling sleepily out of the guest bedroom. Elaine apologized in rusty French for Jack's eruption during Jean-Marc's quality sleep time. Unfortunately for Elaine, her French apology translated as, "I'm happy Jack is a sunny goat." Her foreign guest's inexplicable eye-roll mystified Elaine.

Myrtle added some more sugar to her coffee cup. "Sloan has a crush on Parke, too."

"Well, she's a beautiful woman."

"With hard eyes. Hard, beady little eyes. And that face that just screams WASP. Her nose is pointy enough to pop a balloon. Parke is pushy, bossy, and hateful to everybody."

"She's slender."

"Bony," answered Myrtle.

"And she's in great shape. She must exercise every day."

"She power walks. She pumps her arms way up and down like a chicken."

"It's supposed to be a great alternative to jogging, Myrtle."

"Well, she looks like she's trying to hightail it to the nearest bathroom."

"Silly or not, it obviously works for her. She's very fit," said Elaine wistfully.

"And I'm not sure I'm buying this portrayal of Parke Stockard as evil incarnate. For one thing, she spends a heck of a lot of money to renovate the church. Word is she's funding a new education wing for the Sunday School."

Myrtle snorted. "A desperate and ultimately futile plot to save her immortal soul. Take it from someone who's vastly old and immensely wise that Parke Stockard qualifies as truly wicked. She enjoys getting people's goats."

The hurricane of howling and thumping against the bedroom door resumed. Elaine wasn't following Myrtle's sudden livestock references and was trying to determine if Parke Stockard was still the subject of the conversation without revealing that she'd not been listening attentively the last few sentences.

Myrtle obsessed over minutiae in her life. But so did Elaine, whose ponderous problem for the week was Jack's sudden ability to remove lids from sippy cups. Elaine thought it safest to pick up on the last thread of the conversation that she could remember. "Sloan wouldn't cut your column because of a crush, Myrtle."

"*And* Parke's become the *Bugle*'s biggest advertiser, which apparently obligates Sloan to be her slave for life. Some free press. Just because she's an all-powerful developer *and* realtor. He thinks she's a big-shot since she used to write a society column in New York. Who cares?" Myrtle's gusty sigh cannoned through the phone line, making Elaine cringe and pull the receiver off her ear. "That column kept me busy."

Elaine said hastily, "Well now you'll have your church work keeping you busy, won't you?" All Red needed was his octogenarian mother getting bored again.

Myrtle's voice was steely. "What church work is that?"

"The Altar Guild and Women of the Church. Red mentioned it this morning."

There was a pregnant pause before Myrtle said, "I didn't sign up for Altar Guild. And certainly not for Women of the Church. Bunch of old biddies. Did *Red* sign me up?"

Elaine would have recognized the danger signs in her mother-in-law's tone if Jack hadn't continued his noisy vigil outside her bedroom door. "Hmm."

Myrtle fumed. "Parke Stockard *was* the best candidate for Bradley, North Carolina's 'Most Likely to be Murdered.' But Red may have beaten her out."

JOSH TUCKER WATCHED as his boss at the *Bradley Bugle*, Sloan Jones, slammed his telephone down. "Good *God*," groaned Sloan, clutching his head. "Deliver me from conversations with Myrtle Clover."

"Still griping about her column getting cut?"

"Well, it's not like I cut it *out*. I just reduced it. It was getting pretty weird, anyway, with all the nosebleed tips lately."

"What's behind cutting *my* piece in the last edition? It wasn't weird at all," said Josh.

"Sorry about that," Sloan said, "Fine writing, as usual. Had to squeeze in Parke's column, though. Her full-page weekly ad took our bookkeeping out of the red. Thank God she pays in advance."

Josh's perfunctory smile disappeared in the deep lines in his face. Sloan went on, "And she's not a bad writer, either. Imagine—two former New York writers on the *Bugle* staff!"

Josh lifted a beefy hand and smoothed it over his high forehead. There were times he missed New York. He'd expected his hometown to change while he was gone, but hadn't noticed any changes at all. Chili dogs were still 99 cents at Bo's Diner. The Bradley Library hadn't circulated any new titles since 1985 and Miss Hudgins still shushed the patrons. The *Bradley Bugle* still considered bridge games and golden anniversaries major local news stories. His mother still fussed over him and brought him watery chicken noodle soup whenever he sniffled. Thomas Wolfe had obviously never visited Bradley, North Carolina, if he thought you could never go home again.

"Parke sure gives the *Bugle* some pizzazz." Sloan dreamily reflected on Parke Stockard's finer qualities, basking again in the radiant smile she'd blindsided him with early that morning. Sloan had carefully combed over his wispy hair today. This task involved locating his comb— a major undertaking, considering it had been misplaced for weeks.

Josh flushed. Parke's expensive floral perfume still cloyingly invaded the newsroom, lingering in his nostrils and firing up his migraines. The scent conjured up Parke's condescending smiles. "Just as long as the copy cutting stops there. We've made an award-winning newspaper, Sloan. The *Bradley Bugle* is starting to get some real attention from the public...and not just the town of Bradley. We don't need her interference."

Sloan smiled fondly at the large, pedestalled trophy of an oversized plumed pen that sat in a place of honor on his paper-congested desk. "Yes, we've done well, haven't we?" Sloan beamed at Josh. His jowly face fell when Josh remained grim. Sloan pulled at his shirt collar. "Space is at a premium, you know. Parke's ad revenue is helping us out a lot, but we're not on a *New York Times* budget. Or even a *Charlotte Observer* budget. Or even a—"

"Point taken. But there's got to be something else you can cut back on. Rita's recipes?"

"I'd get reader hate mail."

"The horoscopes Maisy Perry makes up?"

"Josh, there're people who plan their whole day around those things. There'll be pandemonium in the streets if Maisy doesn't give them some guidance."

"Well then, the 'Good Neighbors' column. If somebody wants to trade their grandma's punch bowl for a few heirloom tomato plants, the *Bugle* doesn't have to get in the middle of it, does it?"

Sloan stared blankly at him. He'd no idea Josh Tucker had gotten so completely out of touch with Bradley reality during his time in New York. "Now you're just talking crazy. If I don't broker deals between folks trying to trade their *National Geographic* collection for a collection of *Reader's Digest* condensed books, I'll be strung up in the streets. My 75-year-old neighbor, Miss Sissy? She'd be out there booing my butt every time I took my trash out. She's the number one fan of 'Good Neighbors.'"

"We're back to Parke then."

Sloan missed the dark undertone in Josh's voice. "And like I told you, Parke is single-handedly financing the dinky amount of copy we *do* have. No, it's got to be your articles and Miss Myrtle's tips. You're winning us awards," added Sloan hastily, "but you can be edited down a little. Miss Myrtle's column is new enough that her readers aren't totally rabid fans yet."

Josh crouched back over his article to signal the end of the conversation. He wasn't going to play second fiddle to Parke Stockard in the newsroom—he didn't care how much ad copy she bought.

TANNER HAYES SPLUTTERED wordlessly, perspiration standing in beads on his high forehead. The fact that his usually ruddy face was ashen and that he dramatically clutched his chest would have alerted insightful observers to his sudden, vicious heart attack. But Parke Stockard, for all her beauty, money, and shrewdness, wasn't particularly perceptive. Or compassionate. She thought only that his round, balding head, buggy eyes, and strangled utterances reminded her of a toad.

She lazily batted a buzzing fly his way with a manicured hand, curious to see if a long tongue would slurp it up. When it didn't, she bored with her flight of fancy and returned to the business at hand.

"Your house," she repeated loudly. Was the old man deaf or just stupid? "You need to sell it to me. Let me know when you're ready to sign on. You'll be amazed how much your property will be worth when we level your house and build three in its place. And really—your home is completely outdated." She waved her slender arm dismissively towards the old Colonial. "You won't have a hope of selling it when you or your wife goes to a nursing home. Which," she pointed out, "could be any day now." She gave him a hard look, spun on her heel, and walked briskly to her car.

As Parke zipped down the road in her sporty car, she angled the rearview mirror down to apply more red lipstick. This explains why she never saw Tanner Hayes lying on his cement driveway, still clutching his chest, or his wife, Althea, hurrying down the long drive to her husband's side.

It was a short drive to her own home. It was an old farmhouse with a wrap-around porch. At least, it was until she'd razed it. Now it was a fabulous Mediterranean-style villa named *Shangri-La* with real stucco, a tiled roof, and an in-law suite in the basement. The in-law suite was sort of a dungeon, but it hardly mattered since Parke had divorced the pesky husband and equally irritating in-laws.

She began to wonder, however, if she should put her son Cecil in the dungeon suite. Perhaps under lock and key. She wasn't sure where all the money she funneled him was going, but if the unsavory tattooed friend with the odd piercings was any indication, Cecil was once again heading down the wrong road. It would be nice to avoid rehab this time. Parke wondered if they even had rehab centers in the South.

She was just pulling the massive wooden front door shut behind her when she heard Cecil's voice echoing through the granite-floored foyer from the balcony above. She whipped off her Chanel sunglasses, ready for battle. What would it be this time? $25,000? $40,000? Bracing herself, she put a tanned hand where she imagined her heart might be. Her son thought she looked as if she was about to recite the Pledge of Allegiance.

"Yes, Cecil," she asked in a faux faint voice. It was a faded enough tone to give Cecil pause.

"Mother, I need a little money." His mind raced, calculating how little he could get away with asking.

"Yes, Cecil?" She sank dramatically into a Chippendale chair, rummaging in her bag for her checkbook.

"Just..." he stopped. "Just....five thousand."

Parke stopped short. Five thousand? Five thousand what? Surely not dollars. There had to be a catch. Five thousand pounds? Five thousand rubies? She wasn't going to give him a chance to revise it. She snatched the checkbook and a pen out of the bag and scribbled out a check, chipping a lacquered nail in the process. She slapped it wordlessly on a marble-topped table in the foyer and swept out of the room. Cecil thoughtfully watched as her high heels tapped out of the foyer. He hoped his free-loading days weren't drawing to a close.

BENTON CHAMBERS PUFFED a cigar (a habit cultivated because he thought that's what Southern politicians were supposed to do). After flicking off the long row of ash, he set the cigar down on a heavy ashtray and pulled open his desk drawer for his flask of Jim Beam and a glass. His pudgy fingers clamped around the flask as he poured the brown liquid into the glass and downed it eagerly, wiping a few stray drops off his bloated features with the back of his wrist.

Benton had thought his re-election to the city council would be a cakewalk. Running on the "preserving Bradley's history" platform was a guaranteed winner since everyone was furious about the Stockard woman sticking McMansions on small lots. Everybody in town was railing against her and his win looked like a sure thing.

Benton stared morosely at his drink, then laid it down and picked up the cigar again. He'd thought serving on the city council would be an easy job. How hard could it be to govern a small Southern town with a quaint and vibrant downtown, a pretty lake, and a healthy tourism industry? If only he'd known. He hadn't counted on Parke coming after *him*, pressuring him. He thought they'd had a totally different arrangement. Who knew someone so beautiful could be so toxic? Blackmailing harpy. And now he was stuck—if he suddenly changed platforms, he'd look like a fool at best and would lose the election at worst. How could he get Parke Stockard to stop talking? He'd put in the time, shook the hands, shot the bull. He had the pretty wife, the friends with beach houses. He'd be a monkey's uncle if that pretty Yankee was going to take him down just when he'd made it big. His cell phone bleated and he ignored its ring after seeing his wife's number on the display. He smoked and thought while the air turned blue.

THE METHODIST MINISTER, Nathaniel Gluck, summoned all his Christian patience to deal with the early-morning visitor in his church office. Kitty's hair was pulled up in a bun, but in her agitation, some hair had come loose, giving her a most disheveled look. Seminary covered weddings, funerals, and board meetings. He was quite sure there'd been no mention of hysterical church ladies with mascara rivers running down their faces.

Kitty sopped up her misery with two brand-new boxes of Kleenex and now Nathaniel rummaged desperately through his desk for a travel pack he knew was hiding in there. Kitty trumpeted into the last remaining tissue and Nathaniel fumbled frantically through the drawer until his long fingers grasped the travel pack. He feared Kitty might soon be in need of a hug and the gangling man felt ill-equipped to handle the puddling mess she'd become.

What had Kitty been talking about before the floodgates opened? "So summing up your concerns, Kitty?"

"Parke is mean. Parke is bossy. Parke tells me they do it better in New York. Parke hates my flower arrangements. Parke says my chicken casseroles make her puke."

"I understand." Nathanial cut off her litany of loathing and affected a spiritual glow he hoped would transfer to his wretched visitor. She opened her mouth again and he sighed. The glow hadn't worked. He'd have to resort to prayer.

"And her Cecil got my Brian into drugs. Now Brian's at reform school and Parke's son is living high on the hog. It's not *fair*." Kitty swabbed her face with one of the travel tissues, succeeding only in smearing the mascara across her cheeks. "Since Parke moved here, everything has changed. My church work is just as important to me as breathing. You know that. The only time I feel good about myself is when I'm arranging flowers on the altar, or cutting up communion bread. I don't get that feeling at home with Tiny."

Nathaniel repressed a shudder at her husband's name. Tiny was the massive, Neanderthal-like redneck who mowed the church lawn. Yes, she needed to escape her home life as much as possible. But it presented him with quite a dilemma.

Kitty's face puckered up and a few fat tears squeezed out. "She's the prettiest woman in Bradley. But Mama always said 'Pretty is as pretty does.' Parke Stockard would be revolting if she looked like she acts." She heaved a hiccupping sigh and gave a malicious smile at the enticing thought of a disfigured Parke.

No question about it: Kitty was a valuable resource. She plugged away at humdrum church chores that no one volunteered to do. But Parke Stockard had her own good points—deep pockets. Not only did she donate new hymnals, plush carpet, and fresh paint, but she had the skills and drive necessary to energize successful fundraising campaigns. The church *could* use a fresh approach and some younger faces in the congregation . . . and Parke *was* channeling lots of money into church coffers. He sighed.

"Nothing was ever proven, though, was it?" he asked gently. "About Parke's son introducing your son to drugs? And it's good to get a dedicated volunteer in God's house, isn't it? You were doing so much for us, single-handedly, that I always worried about you. Maybe you could take the higher ground and befriend Parke. She's just a newcomer looking for her niche, after all. Won't you prayerfully consider reaching out to her?"

Kitty looked at him sadly. He winced, guessing she must realize the influence Parke's money exerted on him. Kitty pulled her battered pocketbook towards her and stood up. "Brian never used drugs. Never. Not until he started hanging out with

Parke's son. Having a new volunteer is one thing—having a dictator is another." She stomped out of his office, ignoring his entreaties to sit down. Nathaniel wrung his bony hands together. There would be trouble. Of that he was sure.

Chapter Two

A gnome village miraculously mushroomed overnight in Myrtle's yard while Red slept. Ceramic gnome characters, all engaged in a variety of cute activities, graced her front lawn. Elaine walked past her kitchen window. She blinked. "Oh Lord. Your mom's called out the gnome patrol, Red. What did you do?"

"What?" Red pushed the curtain aside. He groaned and pressed his hands against his eyes, hoping when he opened them the image of a hundred ceramic gnomes cluttering his mother's yard across the street would have vanished. He was disappointed.

"Red, what did you *do* to your mother?" asked Elaine. Displaying her gigantic gnome collection in her front yard was Myrtle's favorite way of expressing her displeasure with her son. "It must have taken her all night to drag all those things out of the shed. She could have broken her neck!"

Red turned back around to face the narrowed eyes of his wife, lampooning him with visual darts. "Nothing! I didn't do..." He stopped. "I signed her up for Women of the Church and Altar Guild."

"I thought you said that was *her* idea!"

"She's bored again, Elaine, and you know that means trouble."

"She's won't be all that bad," demurred Elaine.

"She won't? Remember when she wrote the blistering editorial to the *Charlotte Observer*?"

"Which one?" asked Elaine.

"That's what I mean! She goes off half-cocked on some random topic and gets everybody all stirred up."

"Well, we don't live in Charlotte anyway. It's not like people are snickering at us behind our backs at the Piggly Wiggly."

"She's caused plenty of trouble here, too, you know. Remember the uncivil unrest she sparked at Greener Pastures Retirement Home?" demanded Red.

Elaine did. Once when Myrtle visited a friend there, she'd spearheaded a protest against the assigned seating in the dining hall. "At your age you should sit where you please," she'd sniffed. This spawned hurt feelings from those happy with their seating assignments and indignation from those who wanted to sit where they chose. They had to bring in the Methodist minister to mediate.

Red sighed. "Whenever she has too much time on her hands, she worries over the little things in life."

Elaine guiltily remembered her hours obsessing on Jack's sippy cup problem.

"She'll meddle in other people's business—organize sit-ins to protest late garbage pick-up...who knows what she might do with a lot of extra time on her hands? She *could* use that extra time for the community good." Red rationalized.

"Arranging flowers in the sanctuary?"

Red knew he wouldn't win this one. Plus, Elaine looked like she was working herself up into a real snit—one that might carry over into their chicken pot pie supper that evening. Or their "American Idol" snuggling-up-time on the sofa together. Or even...

"What do you want me to do?" he pleaded, palms held up in supplication.

"Apologize to your mother. Send those gnomes packing—before people really *do* snicker at us at the Piggly Wiggly."

Red picked up the cordless phone, which Elaine quickly pulled from his hand and set back onto the counter. She propelled him to the front door, pushed him out, and went back for a second cup of coffee. She was greeted in the kitchen by their half-asleep French exchange student. Jean-Marc shuffled past the kitchen window, stopped short at the sight of the gnomes, and peered through it again. "*Zut alors!*" Elaine wordlessly poured him a large cup of coffee.

Red was too late to patch things up with Myrtle that morning. She was already stomping her way to church for the Altar Guild meeting he'd gotten her into. Myrtle's cane thumped emphatically on the pavement in front of her, the robustness of the sound giving her a sense of satisfaction. The skin that stretched over her big bones were wrinkle-free...just a few fine lines when she smiled and frowned. She was tall and cut an imposing figure in the classroom where she'd reigned supreme for twenty-five years before retiring more years ago than she cared to remember. She smiled smugly at the thought of her gnome army greeting

Red this morning. If she'd *wanted* to get involved with Altar Guild and Women of the Church, she'd have signed up herself.

Altar Guild was synonymous with Parke Stockard, who seemed bent on taking over every church activity she could get involved with. Great. A morning with Parke certainly wouldn't cure Myrtle's foul mood. She gave her cane another vicious whack on the sidewalk, then pushed through the heavy wooden doors into the sanctuary, checking her murderous thoughts at the door. Although someone clearly hadn't checked theirs.

Parke Stockard lay sprawled at the altar, sightless eyes wide open. For once, Myrtle was glad to have her cane to lean on.

"Miss Myrtle! Here to help us out with Altar Guild?" The minister, Nathaniel Gluck, loped into the sanctuary, long arms dangling awkwardly by his sides. He blanched when he spotted the body by the altar, stopping in his tracks. Nathaniel moved forward, then stopped again. His bony hands clutched his throat and he made a choking, gasping sound before getting back in control. "Merciful heavens! Oh..." he wheezed a trembling sigh, "dear. Miss Myrtle, we should leave. Should phone the police. Or an ambulance. My office is just down the hall..." His hands flapped helplessly in the air like a scrawny fledgling trying to fly off.

Myrtle had no intention of being shepherded away. "Don't worry about *me*, Nathaniel. I'll just—um—stay here and make sure the crime scene isn't tampered with. Parke's days of needing ambulances are long gone. Just call Red." Myrtle's son Red was Bradley's chief of police. The minister scuttled off to his office.

The crime scene had a film noir feel to it. The pulpit cast creepy shadows over the dead blonde on the floor. Even the blood spatters had an artful feel about them, with Parke's stray hairs matted down just so. Roses lay scattered on the altar, on Parke, and on the floor, a subtle reminder of the violent act. The only odd thing was—Myrtle squinted in disbelief—Parke's knit top was on inside-out. How very un-Parkelike.

Her body sprawled dramatically in front of the altar with a broken crystal vase lying in splinters nearby. Myrtle moved closer, wondering what kind of information she could pick up before Red came roaring over in his squad car and hustled her out of there as fast as she could toddle.

Shocked by her daring, Myrtle bent down and placed a hand on Parke's bare arm. Her body was still warm. The murder had been very recent.. The hush of the sanctuary took on a more sinister feel and the hairs on the back of Myrtle's neck stood on end.

Parke obviously died from blunt force trauma. But what weapon had the killer used? The altar was a mess and the weapon could be almost any of the heavy objects lying on it or nearby. Had the crystal vase smashed on Parke's head or on the floor during a struggle? A heavy brass collection plate could easily have been the weapon. Or the huge, brass-footed candlesticks that lay overturned on the altar.

Myrtle leaned closer to investigate blood on the collection plate, and noticed a cell phone nearly obscured by the avalanche of roses. Putting down her cane, she took a tissue from her pocketbook and picked up the phone. "Good Myrtle" argued against tampering with evidence. That was until "Bad Myrtle" pointed out she had a God-given talent for solving puzzles. Crosswords, true, but they could be just as cryptic as murders. She was *assisting* the police. "Good Myrtle" kept quiet.

Myrtle scrolled through the phone's menu until she got to the call log. Parke Stockard sure had lots of numbers on her contact list, but Myrtle doubted they were all friends. Recent calls included Althea Hayes, Benton Chambers, and Josh Tucker, her co-worker at the *Bradley Bugle*. She tried listening to the voicemail messages, but hung up with disappointment when prompted for a password. She eased the phone back where she'd found it and sat down in a pew to wait for Nathaniel. Still looking around, she spotted a large Bible a couple of feet away from her—definitely not a pew Bible, judging from the papers and sticky notes protruding from it. She slid across the wooden pew, opened the book, and saw Kitty Kirk's name written in loopy, schoolgirl cursive in the front of the Bible.

She snapped the Bible shut when the door opened and sat demurely as Nathaniel entered the sanctuary. "Red's on his way," he said. The minister glanced at the body and sighed. Wrinkling his brow, he gingerly stepping up to the altar. "Odd," he said.

"What is?"

"The flowers. I don't remember roses in the arrangement this morning." He frowned. "We have a member with a terrible allergy to roses and Kitty is always so careful to avoid using them." He seemed about to continue, then stopped short.

"I never dreamed she'd be murdered," he said in a hushed tone, almost to himself.

"Were you worried something like this might happen?"

He shook his head emphatically. "Nothing like this. I'd have told Red if I thought any harm would come to Parke. But she didn't have many fans, I'm afraid."

Myrtle scowled in remembrance. "I'm not surprised."

"But her heart was in the right place," he insisted.

"I just remember that Dorothy Parker quote. *'If you want to know what God thinks of money, just look at the people he gave it to,'*" said Myrtle.

Nathaniel smiled noncommittally and continued an anxious vigil over the body. Discovering the body of the church's biggest benefactor capped off the worst week he'd ever had at the church. He'd received phone calls all week complaining about the new hymnals that Parke Stockard had donated. Last Sunday's service featured the hymn "God of Our Fathers." In an effort at political correctness, the modern hymnal had diplomatically changed the words to "God of the Ages," much to the apparent displeasure of most of the congregation.

Myrtle sniffed the air suddenly. She hadn't immediately noticed in the flurry of discovering Parke's body, but she was certain she smelled cigarette smoke in the sanctuary. She pictured a stubble-jawed, bald tough guy with a cigarette dangling out of the corner of his sneering mouth, easily murdering Parke with one hand tied behind his back for good sportsmanship. But the smell was too faint for someone to have been smoking in the room. More likely the killer had been smoking previously and Myrtle smelled the traces of smoke from his clothing. It confirmed that Parke hadn't been dead for very long.

The wail of a siren, the sound of gravel crunching as a car swiftly pulled into the church parking lot, and a door slamming interrupted their conversation. A minute later, Myrtle's son, the town of Bradley's police chief, hurried in with one of his two deputies behind him. The hair that had given Red his nickname was now heavily sprinkled with gray, which he attributed to worrying over his mother, rather than the fact that he was in his late forties. His tough look was enhanced by a jagged scar that snaked down the side of his face. Red liked everyone to assume it came answering the call of duty, but the scar actually involved a homemade bike ramp, a helmetless Red, and some eight-year-old friends egging him on. His green eyes briefly swept over the murder scene, halting at the sight of Myrtle.

"Mama!" His face flushed. "Are you determined to screw up my day? First a return to gnome-land followed by discovering murdered bodies in churches?"

"Well, somebody had to discover the body, Red. At least you know I'm not a suspect."

Red looked menacing, which wasn't difficult considering his big-boned six-foot four inch frame. "I'm not so sure I do know that, Mama. Seems like I remember Elaine telling me about your beef with Parke Stockard."

Myrtle bristled. "Not a *beef*. A—disagreement." Her yard gnomes would be camping out for a while.

Red turned to look at the body once again. "I've put out a call to the state police. And I need to get both of y'all out of the way and get your statements from you."

Myrtle slowly moved towards the door, looking around her as she walked.

"Get a move on, Mama."

"Don't be in such a hurry, Red," she responded huffily. "I need to get my cane."

Red looked around, squinting his green eyes. "Well, where is it? It *should* be in your hand. Or if not, it *should* be right by the sanctuary door. Right?" He took a deep breath to control his temper, strode over a yard from Parke's body, and picked up Myrtle's cane. "Because we don't interfere with crime scenes, do we?"

"For heaven's sake. I was just getting close to make sure the poor woman wasn't still alive and needing an ambulance."

Red snorted. "I hardly think there was any doubt as to her vitals, or lack of them." He grabbed her cane from the pew near Kitty's Bible and herded Myrtle towards the sanctuary door where Nathaniel was still anxiously hovering. His hand tightened on Myrtle's arm and she looked up to see a figure ducking out of sight through the door.

"Hey! Stop—police!" bellowed Red, as he and his deputy moved swiftly towards the exit. A moment later, Althea Hayes appeared, well-dressed in a pale green jacket and flowing green skirt. She put a trembling hand to her mouth when she saw Parke's body. Althea's white hair was wound, as always, neatly in the back of her head in what Myrtle supposed was a French twist, kept in place by a tortoiseshell clip. Myrtle was very envious of Althea's hair: it was thick and well-behaved. Fine and uncooperative in her youth, Myrtle's hair had become wispily contrary in her old age. She tamed it with monthly perms that only succeeded in running more of her hair off. Despite Althea's breathless appearance in the sanctuary, only a couple of tendrils had escaped her French twist. Myrtle was sure she must resemble

Einstein again by now—she'd run her hand through her hair so many times since discovering Parke's body.

"Mrs. Hayes," said Red with surprise. "What are you doing here?"

"I—," Althea started, then swallowed hard, looking towards the body in front of the altar. "I'm here for the Women of the Church meeting."

"That would be over in the dining hall, though, wouldn't it?"

Nathaniel Gluck stepped in. "Well, it is, but I'm sure Mrs. Hayes was just checking on the floral display, weren't you? Because you and Kitty Kirk share Altar Guild duties." He looked searchingly at Althea's face.

Althea nodded weakly, still looking towards the body.

Red looked at her with a direct gaze. "Mrs. Hayes, did you see or hear anyone when you came into the church?"

Althea shook her head vehemently. She's hiding something, thought Myrtle.

"Come on now," said Red briskly, "we need to get away from the crime scene. I need to make a phone call, then I'll need statements from all of you. It might be better if I get them at the station, since the forensic guys are going to need to check out the church."

"And find the fingerprints and DNA of everyone in the town," Myrtle said.

"What the—" Red spluttered as what sounded like a parade of cars and people outside the church. Striding to the stained glass window, he peered through a red panel. Red started uttering a curse, which he hastily changed into "Jiminy Cricket!" as he remembered he was in church. "The whole town of Bradley is out there."

"Can't blame anyone but yourself and those sirens," said Myrtle, carrying herself regally out the church door.

The scene outside resembled a paparazzi free-for-all. There were what looked like *all* the usual church ladies, some still in housecoats and curlers. Josh Tucker, *Bradley Bugle* reporter, was taking pictures and sneezing emphatically. In between sneezes and coughs, he juggled his digital camera and made notes. Kitty Kirk, the leader of the church ladies, appeared especially peculiar and her complexion looked almost gray. She stared oddly at the reporter. Myrtle figured it must be because Erma Sherman, Myrtle's nosy next-door neighbor, had just plowed through the crowd and leeched onto Josh Tucker's camera arm, gabbing and gazing fatuously into Josh's nervous eyes. Myrtle guessed he didn't return Erma's affection: he was pasty-white and carefully ignoring her while still in the throes of a sneezing fit. Maybe he was allergic to her.

Erma's braying laugh and large front teeth combined to give her an unfortunate resemblance to a donkey. Her medical afflictions were legion and eagerly shared with others. Whatever her ailments, her eyesight and hearing were excellent, much to the frustration and dismay of Myrtle as she tried to stealthily slip by her. Remembering the cigarette smoke, she edged closer to Josh and Erma and sniffed delicately. She smelled nothing and wandered slowly through the crowd, sniffing as she went, to no avail. Her olfactory mission was cut short when Red's booming voice cracked like a whip over the crowd. "Everyone will retreat to their cars and return wherever they were before they came here. This is a *crime scene.*"

This statement prompted a thrilled gasp from some of the church ladies, but with one look at Red, they decided to forgo an inquisition. Reluctantly, they filed back to their cars, the reporter from the *Bugle* still taking pictures and sneezing with Erma Sherman matching him step for step.

"If you'll go ahead and get in the cruiser, Mama," said Red, "we'll go to the station and I'll get your statement from you there. Let me talk with Nathaniel for just a minute and I'll be right with you. The state police is coming over and Detective Lieutenant Perkins will want to talk with you."

"John Perkins is assigned to the case? Well, at least it's someone I know."

Red raised his eyebrows. "That's right...I'd forgotten. We'd had you over for dinner when he was here on police business? I'm surprised you even remember him."

She started to answer but Red quickly walked off. Myrtle remembered Detective Lieutenant Perkins well. She'd tried to pump him for information over dinner on a high-profile murder case that was splashed all over the news. He was a nice enough man—except for the fact that he gave away absolutely *nothing.* He made the Buckingham Palace guards look animated.

Myrtle hoped he wouldn't prove so stoic this time. Solving the case before Red or the state police would prove a point and get back at Red for his high-handed treatment of her.

MYRTLE EASED INTO THE front seat of the cruiser to wait for Red. If she got in the backseat, it would be all over town that Myrtle Clover murdered Parke Stockard. Not that Parke hadn't had it coming.

The trip to the station took only a couple of minutes with Red behind the wheel. Myrtle spotted a group of locals sitting on a wooden bench outside the diner as Red pulled up in front of the old, brick courthouse that housed the police station and city hall. Word traveled fast in Bradley, North Carolina.

"Vultures," Myrtle spat out.

"Mama, those old guys are *always* outside Bo's Diner. Every morning they get their coffee and sit around in their golf caps, shooting the bull and cutting-up. It's got nothing to do with the murder."

"They usually don't have their cackling crones with them."

"Cackling...? Their wives, you mean? They're probably just enjoying another relaxing morning of retirement with their husbands."

Myrtle noticed the old women lean closer and turn up their hearing aids hopefully as she and Red entered the police station. She really couldn't blame them too much for their interest. Bradley, North Carolina, population 1,500, wasn't ordinarily a murder magnet. Crime waves had formerly consisted of Bud Dickens and Crockett Scott getting sloshed several nights in a row and loudly warbling Willie Nelson songs in the streets.

Red held open the weather-beaten wooden door for his mother and she walked into the tiny police station, stepping carefully so she wouldn't lose her footing on the warped pinewood floors that groaned in protest where she trod.

Following standard procedure, Red notified the state police as soon as he'd gotten the call from the minister about the murder. As Red poured her a Coca-Cola, some of the forensics team had already arrived in town and checked in at the station before stopping at the church.

The door opened to a tall, wiry man with a super-short military haircut. Detective Lieutenant Perkins greeted her in his polite, measured way. Myrtle decided to override his reserve with an exuberant hug. Best to knock him off-guard to maybe squeeze some information out of him. He gave an "oof" from the ferocity of her embrace, but appeared to be onto her as he watched her with appraising eyes.

"Mrs. Clover," he said. He led her into Red's small office and closed the door. "It's nice to see you even if the circumstances aren't as pleasant as last time. Could you go over what led you to the church this morning and what happened when you got there?" He picked up a notebook and pen from Red's desk.

Myrtle took a deep breath and outlined the day's events, going into great depth when describing Red's busybody meddling in her personal life and the horrors of Women of the Church and Altar Guild duty. She described the moment she'd discovered Parke Stockard with melodrama and sound effects, and carefully omitting clues she'd seen there, or her perusal of Parke's cell phone. Finishing her monologue, she neatly folded her hands in her lap and waited for his reaction. No reaction was forthcoming, though, as Perkins carefully replaced the cap on his ballpoint pen and tapped it gently against the notebook.

"Tell me why you think this might have happened, Mrs. Clover. Why would Parke Stockard, by all accounts a philanthropic benefit to the town of Bradley, have been murdered in the very place she spent so much time and money?"

Myrtle paused. It made no sense to help Perkins with his investigation when she was trying to solve the case herself. He should do his own poking and prodding.

Lieutenant Perkins said, "It would be a tremendous help, Mrs. Clover, if you shared your opinion with me. You obviously have a lot of useful insights which could help point us in the right direction."

Finally someone who valued her opinions. But that didn't mean she had to help him out. Besides, she didn't really *know* anything. "I'm afraid I've no idea, Detective." Perkins frowned and she hastily added, "Poor Parke." But it didn't sound very convincing.

He snapped shut his notebook and stood up. "Thanks, Mrs. Clover. If you think of anything else, be sure to let Red know." At Myrtle's grimace, he amended, "Or call me, instead." He handed her his business card and respectfully waited for her to pull out of the deep office chair, but didn't belittle her by trying to help. She wondered if Red had smelled the cigarette smoke in the sanctuary. But he'd been so bent out of shape with her for discovering a body that he probably hadn't noticed anything else.

Judging from Red's expression as she tottered back into the station lobby, he was still pretty irritated. He offered to drive her back home. At least, that's what she *thought* he said. It was hard to hear words coming out from gritted teeth.

They drove off. Myrtle glanced at her watch. "Just in time to catch *Tomorrow's Promise*."

Red gave a short laugh. "Elaine called to check on you a little while ago. I'll call her back and let her know you're doing okay after all. Discovering murdered bodies is all in a day's work—you've already moved on to your soap opera."

"*Tomorrow's Promise* has a storyline that's eerily similar and could provide some interesting perspective, Red. Angelique infuriates everyone on the soap—but she's bipolar and can't really help it, bless her heart. Cliff snarls at the camera and plots mischief because Angelique's ex-husband is his brother and she's stalking him because he's dating Cliff's sister-in-law but just got her pregnant—"

"And this is like Parke's murder *how*, exactly?"

"Because Angelique was killed, of course. Why else?"

Red's fingers gripped the steering wheel tightly as he pulled into Myrtle's driveway.

"You should see a doctor about that nervous tic, Red. And all your veins are standing out on your forehead, too. Hope it doesn't mean high blood pressure." With that final word, Myrtle climbed out of the patrol car and slammed the door shut behind her. Picking her way carefully around the gnomes, she walked to her front door as Red's car roared off.

Chapter Three

The buck-toothed, one-eared bunny crack on the ceiling mocked Myrtle's insomnia. Altar Guild had been the final straw. Myrtle glared at the rabbit. The *gall* of Red. And all the jokes he'd been making about farming her out to Greener Pastures Retirement Home. There was no way he was putting her out to pasture. Just because she drove him a little crazy—as if he hadn't contributed to all her gray hairs when he was a teen.

Kicking the covers off, Myrtle pulled herself upright and padded into the kitchen for her obligatory nightcap of warm milk. There was no point in staying in bed with nothing to do but study that crack in the ceiling and mull over the way the overhead light fixture resembled a pug-nosed alien. She sat down at her kitchen table and schemed to solve the case before Red and Perkins could uncover the first clue. It couldn't be much of a stretch to go from crosswords to crime: figuring out clues, making educated guesses, erasing mistakes and starting over. It was a cinch.

Myrtle pulled her grocery list towards her and tore off the top page. She jotted down a list of questions. Why was Althea Hayes in the sanctuary? Who was the mystery smoker? Did the flower arrangement change have anything to do with the murder? Had Kitty Kirk recently left her Bible in the pew, or had it been sitting there since last Sunday? And...who wanted to kill Parke Stockard?

Well, who *didn't* want to murder her? She'd just recently put herself on Myrtle's own hit list. Parke Stockard was bossy and liked things done her own way. She was beautiful and flaunted it. She played people off each other for fun and maybe even for profit. People were sick and tired of her and she hadn't even lived in Bradley all that long.

She wrote down the names she'd found on Parke's cell phone: Althea, Benton Chambers, and Josh Tucker. She drained the last of her milk and looked over the notes. She was going to do it. Solving the case would flex her brain and prove she still had the brainpower—more than even Red himself, if she beat him to it.

Myrtle was still mulling the case over the next morning while she spooned globs of garlic and handfuls of shredded cheese into a pot of grits. The challenge would be interviewing the suspects. Well, besides figuring out who the suspects *were*, of course. Casually knocking at their doors and grilling them on their alibis wouldn't cut it. Once they'd tattled to Red, all her fun would be over. There had to be a better, more surreptitious way to ask some questions. Thinking hard, she'd stopped stirring the grits and they spat at her angrily. Myrtle gave them a quick stir and then took them off the eye completely when the phone rang.

"Elaine! Everything going well over there?" Myrtle couldn't hear any crying on the other end. It was a good sign, unless it indicated that Elaine had run away from home.

"It's great, actually. I've got some free time since Jack is over at a playdate."

Myrtle smiled. Would she finally get a sounding board? A Watson? Detectives were supposed to have sidekicks.

"I thought we could go to book club together. It'll do you good to get out after the day you had yesterday. I can pick you up in about 45 minutes."

Myrtle's bubble burst. "But I haven't read the book."

"It's *To Kill a Mockingbird.*"

"Oh. Right." She'd taught it for fifteen years at school. Now Red was enlisting Elaine to 'get Mama's mind off the murder.' Myrtle avoided Elaine's book club like the plague because they considered trashy paperbacks serious literature. They could collectively author a reference guide titled: *Book Picks for Chicks: An Exhaustive Collection of Trendy Tripe.* This had to be the first time they'd ever picked anything with any literary merit.

"The problem with your book club, Elaine—besides the crummy books—are all the loud-mouths. Every occasion with those women descends into a big brag-fest."

"You're exaggerating again, Myrtle."

"Think about it, Elaine. Libby Holloway is always bragging about her freakishly large tomatoes."

"Which she generously shares with the club."

"You've got Margaret Goodner's Stepford grandchildren who speak in tongues..."

"They speak six perfectly *normal* languages."

"And Heather Herbert's nasty toy dog that she inbreeds with all its award-winning relatives."

"Apparently the best way to ensure blue ribbons at dog shows."

"And Erma Sherman is in your club. Enough said."

"You're leaving out all the best people, Myrtle. Tippy Chambers, Althea Hayes, Kitty Kirk..."

Myrtle *had* forgotten about them. And they were gossipy people who disliked the now-very-dead Parke Stockard. An about-face was in order.

"That might be a good idea, Elaine. I'll be ready when you swing by."

But her about-face was perhaps a bit abrupt. Elaine paused. "Okay, I don't know who you are, but put Myrtle Clover back on the phone."

Myrtle tittered. "Funny, funny Elaine. You just convinced me to change my mind, that's all."

"All right. I'll pick you up in ten minutes." Elaine had a surprised lilt to her voice. She likely wondered if Myrtle's change of heart could be attributed to a mild stroke.

When Myrtle stepped into Elaine's car, she lifted her eyebrows in surprise at Elaine's messy hair and tracksuit. With her usually smooth black bob, tidy appearance, and measured response to the chaos around her, Myrtle considered Elaine a great asset to the chaotic Clover family. Rumpled and scattered, Elaine was a shadow of her former, highly functioning self. Seeing some flaws sure made it easier to feel sorry for her, though. She seemed....well, more like a normal person. But not like a promising sounding board for Myrtle. They both pretended not to see the gnomes still invading Myrtle's front yard.

"Oh," said Elaine, "I tried to call your cell phone yesterday afternoon and see how you were doing. Did you have it turned off?"

"That stupid thing holds a charge for about 5 minutes before it dies."

"Well, you've had it for five years, which is practically prehistoric for a cell phone. Want me to pick you up another one?"

"Would you? Those kinds of stores make me break out in hives. Buy the most basic phone you can find. I don't want to take pictures with it, I just want to get phone calls."

"I'll try to get one this afternoon."

Myrtle peered at the huge expanse of sky visible through the minivan windshield. "Oops. Bad weather coming."

"Did you catch the forecast this morning?"

"No, no. The sky is red, don't you see it? 'Red in morning, sailors take warning.'"

Elaine looked worried now. First Myrtle voluntarily agreed to go to book club, now she was babbling about sailors. That stroke seemed like more of a possibility now.

The book club meeting was at Tippy Chambers' house this week. Although it wasn't a long drive, it was fraught with peril as Elaine simultaneously drove the car, answered two cell phone calls, and scrubbed at a spot on her pants. Myrtle gripped the door with white-knuckled hands through the ordeal, gratefully stepping onto terra firma when the car finally stopped outside the Chambers' house.

If you resurrected Scarlet O'Hara and transplanted her to North Carolina, she'd room with Tippy Chambers and not spare a thought for Tara. Not only was the columned house elegant and historic, it also boasted all the bells and whistles that Parke Stockard was so crazy about. The mature landscaping of massive magnolias masked the house from the street.

Tippy, well-dressed as usual with white slacks and a silk, lime-green blouse, greeted them at the door. Her carefully arranged blonde coif didn't have a hair out of place. Still, Myrtle thought she looked tired this morning and every bit of her 50-plus years. She was perfectly organized, perfectly dressed, perfectly coiffed, and gave perfect parties, but her heart didn't seem to be in it. Myrtle wondered if she were just going through the motions. And whether Tippy knew of her husband's affairs.

"Miss Myrtle, it's so good to have you here. You're a real feather in my cap—we've been dying for Elaine to bring you along and give our discussions some direction. An English teacher is just what we needed," said Tippy politely.

"Well, I haven't taught for a while, Tippy. But I'm...uh...glad to help." Once an English teacher, always an English teacher. Even if you've been retired for twenty years. You never knew when you'd be drafted back to serve a tour of duty at some random book club meeting.

Passing through the oriental rug-lined foyer, Myrtle peered hopefully into the living room. She smiled when she spotted both Althea Hayes and Kitty Kirk. The smile turned to a grimace when she saw the rodent-like countenance of her neighbor, Erma Sherman. But between Tippy, Althea, and Kitty, Myrtle was sure she could dig up some dirt. Leaning on her cane as she walked, she entered the antique-filled, book-lined living room and settled on a settee. There was a good-sized group of about twelve women there, probably due to the interest in gossip about the murder.

While she engaged in a little preliminary small-talk and graciously managed self-deprecating smiles when everyone chirped up about how exciting it was to have an English lit teacher with them, she took mental notes on the appearance and demeanor of her quarry.

Althea Hayes looked as tidy as ever but made a peculiar fashion statement in a wool sweater over her linen pants. She avoided Myrtle's eyes. Did Althea have a beef with Tippy's thermostat settings, or were nerves making her shiver? She was always a no-nonsense type, but looked particularly grim this morning. But then, Myrtle reminded herself, she'd buried her husband just a few days ago. She probably needed a distraction.

Kitty Kirk was a train wreck. Whatever good Samaritan had dragged her god-forsaken carcass out of bed to book club should be shot. This was a woman who needed to be put out of her misery, not force-fed literature in a mansion. Kitty, who usually appeared immaculate, seemed to have foundation on only one side of her face, giving her the peculiar look of an uneven suntan—as if she'd fallen asleep on a lounge at the pool and woken up much later. Her eyeliner had missed its target and looked more like the stuff football players smear under their eyes. A wayward toddler seemed to have applied her lipstick. She usually wore a cute boutique-y outfit with carefully chosen, if rather loud, chunky jewelry. But today she wore a muumuu of the type generally purchased from the coupon section of the Sunday newspaper.

Kitty slouched in an antique armchair, squinting at Myrtle when she arrived before drooping down again in disinterest. She looked awful. Myrtle wondered if she could possibly be intoxicated, despite the fact it was 9:30 A.M. Or maybe hung-over from boozing the night before. Looking at her was like watching a train wreck. Myrtle dragged her eyes away with difficulty.

"Today's discussion is on a simply marvelous book that's an old friend to all of us," Tippy said in a let's-get-started voice. Myrtle frowned. No chance to quiz anyone yet. She satisfied her investigative instincts by watching faces in the group and sniffing the air a few times for whiffs of cigarette smoke. Smelling nothing, she loaded up a napkin with cheese and crackers and muffins and settled back as the discussion started. She should have brought her ear plugs. She had a feeling it was going to be bad.

Myrtle snacked on muffins and mulled over the case while the ladies discussed the book. She let completely outrageous statements about To *Kill a Mockingbird* pass without a single eye-roll, deep sigh, or click of her tongue. One member compared the book to *Valley of the Dolls* and another drew a parallel to *Peyton Place*. Someone repeatedly said "metaphor" instead of "analogy." Myrtle kept right on scarfing down appetizers and apple juice.

She was brought back to reality with a thump when Erma Sherman said, "I thought Scout should have been nicer to Bee Radley. He should have knocked on Bee's door right away."

"BOO Radley," hissed Myrtle. "And Scout is a she."

Tippy took Myrtle's grumpy interjection as a sign to wrap up the discussion part of the meeting. "Muffins, anyone?" Since Myrtle had eaten most of the muffins, Tippy quickly started circulating some other appetizers. Myrtle noticed dark circles under her eyes. Maybe Tippy Chambers wasn't as calm and composed as Myrtle first thought.

Myrtle began despairing that the topic of murder would ever come up. Maybe everyone figured Tippy Chambers' elegant living room wasn't the place to introduce the subject of violent death. Myrtle ground her teeth, enduring a conversation about how difficult it was to find a new president for the garden club. She could have kissed clueless Erma Sherman (and Tippy Chambers, judging from her thunderous expression, likely could have killed her) when she breathlessly asked, "When are we going to talk about it? Can you believe Parke Stockard was *murdered*? And I had *just* seen her day before yesterday!"

There was an uncomfortable silence. Myrtle finally said. "Well, of *course* you saw her day before yesterday. She *was* alive then, you know." A nervous tittering of laughter followed. Kitty Kirk's hands clenched in her lap and Althea looked uncharacteristically nervous as she shrank into her chair.

Myrtle adopted a chatty persona. If something weren't done to continue this line of conversation, then someone was going to change the subject. "What a *terrible* thing to have happened. Didn't I say that, Elaine? A *terrible* thing." Elaine looked glum as she was dragged as an unwilling prop into Myrtle's staged conversation. "I wonder who could have done such a thing."

Tippy said briskly, "It's obviously the work of some criminal, Myrtle. Maybe an itinerant worker or some such person."

Erma gave a snorting laugh. "It's not like there weren't enough people around town who wanted to kill her. You don't have to bring in migrant workers." This time she seemed more aware of the deafening silence. "Well, no one liked Parke, after all. Kitty, *you* couldn't *stand* her."

Kitty's tongue worried her lips nervously. "Parke was my friend!"

"She certainly was *not*," said Erma in a belligerent voice. "The whole reason Parke was at the church in the first place was to rearrange the flowers you'd arranged on the altar. You can't exactly be happy that she hated your flower arrangements, Kitty. In fact, you must be a prime suspect." Erma had a mean smile on her face and Myrtle was reminded of a fat cat toying with a garishly made-up mouse.

Kitty started shaking and stuttered like a stalled car while she tried making traction with some words. No luck. Myrtle wondered if she could be having a nicotine fit and sniffed the air again hopefully. Kitty finally managed to spit out, "I'd never get close enough to that woman to kill her! She—" Kitty made a dash for the powder room, muumuu flowing behind her. She ran smack into the door jamb on her way out.

"Blind as a bat," said Erma smugly. "Someone should guide her to the bathroom before she dings a Ming."

"I'll help her," said Myrtle as she left the room in hot pursuit. As hot as the pursuit could be when the pursuer was an octogenarian with a cane. Elaine smiled faintly at her book club and meekly changed the subject, silently cursing Myrtle the entire time.

When Myrtle caught up with Kitty, she was in the downstairs powder room and reapplying eyeliner with a heavy hand. Myrtle dropped into a chair in the powder room and looked around her. "Good Lord, Tippy could have hosted book club in *here*."

Kitty squinted around the room, without bothering to take her coke-bottle glasses out of her bag. "It's pretty big."

"I can't imagine the philosophy behind having a huge powder room with chairs in it. Are we intended to loiter here?"

"Let's do," said Kitty fervently and Myrtle reached forward to squeeze her hand. "Erma is a pill. Just ignore her. *You're* not a suspect, I'm sure. I'm sure you must have a wonderful alibi."

Kitty gave a gulping sob and continued circling her eyes with the eyeliner pencil. As far as Myrtle could tell, most of the liner seemed to be cascading down her face just as soon as she applied it. "That's just the thing, Miss Myrtle. I *was* at the church that morning. Not before Parke died, of course," she added hurriedly. "But for the Women of the Church meeting. And everyone knows I *didn't* like Parke. That sorry son of hers destroyed my boy. Drugs! In Bradley!"

Kitty rooted around in her battered pocketbook until she pulled out a tube of lipstick. Feeling more refreshed, she continued. "Parke was as rotten as her son. She tried to force me out of all my church work. The church is the only place I ever felt I belonged. I've always been *somebody* important at the church: cooking the dinners for Wednesday nights, putting together the flower arrangements. And she took everything over. She made me feel so useless."

Myrtle reached over and squeezed her hand wordlessly for a minute. "I know just how you feel, Kitty. Funny how different things can make you feel useless. I felt bad when Red forced church work down my throat and you were upset you couldn't do more."

Kitty smiled at her. "I knew you were mad about something." Myrtle lifted her eyebrows inquiringly. "I saw the gnomes," Kitty explained.

Myrtle squeezed her hand again. "But I don't understand why you're so upset now, Kitty. After all, as unpleasant as it is, Parke is out of the way. You can resume your jobs at the church and Nathaniel and the congregation will be delighted and relieved."

Kitty's eyes had that hollow look again. "They think I had something to do with it, Miss Myrtle. Like I said, everyone knows I couldn't stand Parke."

"That's no evidence you *murdered* her, Kitty! I was at the church myself that morning and I'm not a suspect."

Kitty paused in the makeup accumulation. Her face now resembled a palate of particularly gaudy paints. She gazed thoughtfully at the toile wallpaper. "That's true," she sniffed and frowned, her brows furrowing. "And I *did* see someone else. Someone hurrying into the church right when I was pulling into the parking lot. I sat in my car talking on my cell phone for a while before I got out. There would have been plenty of time for him to kill Parke and sneak out again before her body was found."

"He?"

"Benton Chambers," whispered Kitty, nervously moistening her dry lips. She squinted fearfully at the powder room door as if expecting to see Tippy Chambers at any moment.

"You're sure about this?" Myrtle asked. Kitty nodded, brown hair flopping on her head. "Did you tell the police about seeing Benton, Kitty?"

"No. I was just so shaken up by the whole thing. And the questions they asked me made me sure they thought I was a suspect. I was so scared that I didn't remember to tell them." She leaned forward and grabbed Myrtle's hand with a tight grip. "Do you think that that's what happened? That Benton Chambers murdered Parke?" She sounded more eager than distraught, Myrtle thought. As if she were grasping at straws.

"You're sure it was Benton Chambers," she pressed.

"Positive. Cocky old son of a gun. Big-bones, leaning on his cane." Myrtle raised her eyebrows in inquiry and Kitty explained, "He had that skiing accident, you know."

"Snow skiing? It's summer!"

"Water skiing. But still."

"What would make Benton do such a thing? Why he would mess up all the good things he's got going for him?"

Kitty shrugged and the purple-flowered muumuu slipped off her shoulder. "Guess it has something to do with him running against development and her being the real estate queen." Kitty moved restlessly from foot to foot. "I guess I should go to the police station and tell them what I saw."

Myrtle was determined to turn in that tidbit herself. Just let Red *try* scoffing at her investigative skills again! "Actually, I'm going over there in a bit myself, so I'll let Red know. Then he can give you a call and save you a trip."

Kitty gratefully squeezed Myrtle's hand. Myrtle felt a twinge of guilt. Kitty said, "I wasn't going to come to the club meeting today, but Tippy drove by and picked me up. Said I needed to get out of the house." Kitty grimaced. "I feel weird around Tippy now, though. With what I saw at the church. Here she was doing something nice for me and the whole time I'm thinking that her husband killed Parke Stockard."

"Let's get back to the others, Kitty. They'll send a search party if we're not back soon." Myrtle also wanted to leave the powder room before Kitty slathered on anymore makeup. It wasn't doing her any favors. Finally, unable to restrain herself anymore, she said, "Here." She pulled a tissue out of her bag, wet it, and quickly scrubbed under Kitty's eyes to get some of the mascara and liner off.

Kitty smiled at her gratefully. Octogenarians could get away with almost anything.

Kitty plodded back to the living room, plopping down onto the sofa. Most of the ladies tactfully continued their conversations and tried to give Kitty time to compose herself, Myrtle noticed. Except for Erma Sherman, of course. She called attention to Kitty by bellowing across the room, "Are you okay?" Myrtle made a growling noise and Elaine loudly asked, "Cough drop, Myrtle?" Kitty pretended not to hear Erma and jumped into animated conversation with a startled Althea Hayes.

Myrtle could scarcely contain herself. Obviously worry about being a suspect had been eating Kitty up inside . . . just look at the woman. Her nerves were shot. Being considered a suspect for Parke's murder had really knocked the stuffing out of her. And now she had information about the murder and it implicated the husband of her friend. No wonder she was in such a state.

The meeting started to break up and Elaine looked eager to leave. Myrtle was still hoping to talk to Althea for a minute. Althea had been so odd in the sanctuary that she was sure she knew something, too. After Myrtle's successful questioning of Kitty, she was impatient to quiz Althea. Unfortunately, Althea seemed to have an inkling of Myrtle's intent and edged closer to the door while trying to divest herself of Erma Sherman, who was intent on finding out more about her adored one, Josh Tucker, Althea's nephew.

Myrtle hovered, barely concealing her impatience as Erma coyly asked, "I'm sure Josh's family must be *so* proud of him? Fancy having a son or nephew who was a *New York Times* reporter!" Looking hemmed in, Althea answered, "Yes, it's been quite a change going to work for the *Bradley Bugle*. But he's still making his parents proud of him, you know. He got that journalism award for the story he wrote on the old mill closing." Finally, she slipped away, much to Myrtle's disappointment. There was a moment at the church, after Myrtle had discovered the body, that Althea had seemed like she knew something. The way she had been behaving was almost...suspicious.

Erma, discovering she was without a victim, lumbered up to Myrtle. As Myrtle looked frantically around for Elaine (who had slipped into the powder room to let Myrtle take her punishment), Erma bellowed, "Seen that new neighbor of ours?"

Myrtle tried to pretend she didn't hear her. She continued her desperate head-craning search for Elaine.

"Miles Standish. That's his name."

Myrtle jerked back to attention. "Ridiculous. It couldn't be."

"It is. Miles Standish."

"No one names their baby after a Pilgrim. No one does."

"His did."

Myrtle angrily shook her head and Erma heaved a fetid sigh that wafted out in a toxic cloud. "He moved into the house just to the other side of me. Just a couple of weeks ago. Did you know?"

Myrtle had not spent much time outdoors while avoiding Erma Sherman's evil clutches, but she'd seen movers unloading a large moving van. And a steady stream of elderly ladies bearing goody baskets.

"Widower, you know," said Erma.

Figured. Available men of a certain age were few and far between in Bradley. Whenever one appeared on the landscape, he was courted—or preyed on—with great ferocity.

"Are you planning on going by to welcome him?" Erma gave her rodent-like grin. "I thought he might be a little young for you, though."

Myrtle leveled a gaze of pure venom at her and roared, "Elaine!" While Elaine tried to extricate herself from a conversation, several ladies came over to talk to Erma.

"Are you talking about the newcomer? I hear that he was a fantastic businessman. A real entrepreneur before he retired!"

"Really?" asked the other, breathlessly. "I thought he'd been an engineer?"

"Engineer like 'choo-choo,' or engineer like "electrical?" asked Erma.

Ninnies! Myrtle reveled in the knowledge that she was above this type of behavior. These women should know that there was an excellent chance that the old gentleman could be half-blind and deaf as a post and want his prospective ladylove to shuttle him all over town. Myrtle already knew the man didn't sleep—every occasion she'd been awake lately (and they had been numerous) she'd noticed the lights on at his house. That's all the neighborhood needed—another insomniac.

"Book club is at my house next time," sang out Erma. "I live right next door to the gnome village."

Everyone looked at Erma sympathetically.

Elaine fortunately presented herself and whisked Myrtle away from the book club meeting in her Cheerio-strewn mini-van. Elaine choked down a chuckle as Myrtle fumed. Erma had really wound her up this time. Distraction was in order.

"So what was going on with Kitty Kirk?"

"Other than the fact she looked like she'd just been dragged out from under a rock?" Myrtle hesitated. Kitty's information on Benton Chambers gave her a real lead she could follow up on. If the police ended up working the same angle, she'd get bumped out of the investigation. Not that she really thought Elaine would confide in Red, but still....

"I—ah—think she's still feeling guilty about Parke Stockard's death. You know, she hated Parke and now she's dead. So she's racked with grief. Or something."

Elaine snorted. "She should be skipping with joy. I'm sure her life is a lot easier without Parke picking apart everything she does. I've always liked Kitty. She's very sweet."

"Sweet enough to give you a toothache. But I did feel sorry for her," said Myrtle grudgingly.

"Especially since she's married to Tiny." Elaine gave a shudder. "What were his parents thinking, naming him Tiny? He's 6'7" and got to be 300 pounds if he's an ounce."

"Maybe because his brain is so tiny? Remember when Kitty took the *Wall Street Journal* just to boggle Tiny's mind with all those numbers higher than ten? I think Kitty's tour of duty with that marriage is about to draw to a close, Elaine. She complains about his redneck behavior so much that she's got to be getting us used to the idea that she might be leaving him."

Kitty had her hands full with Tiny. Tiny didn't go to church or even make it to Sunday School. Tiny drank too much, swore too much, and didn't bathe frequently enough. Tiny either worked too late or not at all. He frequented bars too regularly or didn't go enough. Tiny hunted every weekend and shot everything that moved, even if it wasn't in season. Tiny ran through their money and was a bad example for their son, Brian. Tiny was handy around the house, but couldn't be bothered. Tiny left his dirty socks in the middle of the floor or didn't wear socks at all. Tiny made Kitty miserable. But she never did leave him, which was the puzzlement of Bradley.

Elaine shook her head in amazement over Kitty's trials with Tiny. "They don't even share the same interests. She's always at the church, volunteering with one thing or another. And Tiny wouldn't know where the church was if he didn't mow the grass there. I take it back—I did see him there a couple of Easters ago."

Myrtle nodded. "He pulled at his collar and tie like he was on a short leash."

They sat in silence for a minute, reflecting on Tiny. Then Elaine said curiously, "By the way, have you met that new neighbor of yours yet?"

"Who . . . Miles Standish?" asked Myrtle sourly.

"What?" Now Elaine was looking at Myrtle with concern. "He was a Pilgrim, Myrtle. Anyway, have you met him? He looks pretty cute for an older man."

Myrtle gave her a pained look and didn't deign to answer, leaving Elaine to rummage through her mind for inoffensive conversation topics as she sped home.

That night, Elaine said to Red, "Your mom is playing detective, you know."

Red groaned and pressed his hands against his eyes. "Shoot. I thought she might be messing around with my case. She was pumping Perkins for information today when he was trying to question *her*." He shook his head.

"When she was at book club today—"

"*What*? Miss Book Snob went to your book club? I didn't think she'd lower herself."

Elaine knitted her brows in irritation. "Well, she went. And while she was there, she cornered Kitty Kirk in the powder room for at least 25 minutes. I'm sure she was asking her questions about the case."

Red swore.

"She must have found out something, too, because she mentioned going by the police station tomorrow morning."

"Perkins will think she's a nut!" said Red. "I've got to figure out some kind of diversion for her...some kind of red herring or tangent to send her on. Or else pin a note on her back, warning the general public to steer clear of her and her nosiness. I'll talk to Perkins about it tomorrow. We'll cook something up to keep her busy for a while."

Chapter Four

R ed trudged into the courthouse, and pushed the old wooden door of the police station open with his foot, sloshing hot coffee on himself in the process. Cursing, he grabbed a handful of tissues off his desk and dabbed at the spots. He tossed the coffee-stained tissues in the direction of the wastebasket and missed. He cursed again.

Perkins thought for a minute, eyeing Red's coffee-stained shirt and flustered manner. Red had great perspective on the people in Bradley and good general intuition—when he wasn't so preoccupied. He could use his help on the case. "Something going on, Red?"

Red plopped down on the old vinyl sofas in the station lobby, taking a long drag at the remainder of his coffee. "Elaine told me last night that my mother has been going around asking a lot of questions about the case. And she was trying to get information from you when you were questioning her, too. I guess she thinks she can save the town single-handedly from its vicious killer."

Perkins said in a thoughtful tone, "I don't remember your mom being all that interested, besides just normal curiosity.

Murders don't happen every day here, after all. She's probably just going after the latest gossip is all."

"I'd like to believe that's all it is. But you don't really know my mother."

He stopped talking when the door to the station pushed open and Myrtle walked in. Red rolled his eyes at Perkins in exasperation and walked behind the desk, fumbling with some papers to let Perkins handle their visitor.

Myrtle had thought out different ways to approach the whole Benton Chambers situation. Although the thought of plowing into the police station and bellowing out the identity of the killer was certainly *tempting*, she thought she'd play her cards better than that. She wanted to really impress Red and Lieutenant Perkins and finding out a random tip from a muumuued woman in a powder room wouldn't properly showcase all her analytical skills. She decided she would go to the police station and give them a few of her other observations. See how they reacted. Then she'd really knock them out when she handed them the name of the murderer on a silver platter.

"Mrs. Clover," said Perkins in a cautious voice. "Did you forget to include something in your statement the other day?"

"Nothing I forgot, Lt. Perkins. But I did want to tell you something I'd noticed and see if you can get to the bottom of it."

Perkins pulled out a small notepad and poised his pencil over the paper. "What did you notice?"

"Kitty is troubled about something."

Lt. Perkins drew his notebook closer and poised his pen. "Did she confide in you, Mrs. Clover?"

Myrtle nodded sagely. "Oh yes. But you could tell she was incredibly preoccupied even before she spoke to me. She said it's because she thought y'all considered her a probable suspect, but there's more to it than that. Her make-up, you know."

"Makeup," Perkins repeated slowly. Red snickered in the background.

Myrtle wagged her finger at him. "Not just her makeup. The muumuu, too."

"Mmm-hmm."

"She usually takes so much care over her appearance you know. Nails. Hair. Cute clothes. A little *too* cutesy for me, but well-kempt."

Perkins closed his eyes for a moment and Myrtle gave him a sharp look. "You should get more sleep, Detective. Anyway, as I was saying, her appearance has really taken a dive lately. Something is on her mind...she knows something about Parke Stockard's murder."

Perkins tuned back in. "Instead of merely being upset by Mrs. Stockard's murder?"

Myrtle snorted. "*No one* was upset by Parke Stockard's murder. You haven't been paying attention. And it occurred to me that Parke Stockard must have been troubled, too."

Perkins winced as he asked, "How did you draw that conclusion?"

"The tag on her clothes." As Perkins stared blankly at her, she leaned in closely. "She had her knit shirt on *inside out*!" She looked at him with the same amazement she'd felt when she'd noticed it. She was about to say, "And wait till I tell you what Kitty saw at the church," when she glimpsed Detective Lieutenant Perkins' face. Well. She'd just keep that little tidbit to herself then if she weren't going to be taken seriously.

Perkins closed his notebook. "Thanks for your help, Mrs. Clover. I'll be sure to have a talk with Kitty Kirk." He imagined the beginning of his interview with her and sighed. *"Now Mrs. Kirk, about these tacky muumuus..."*

Perkins disappeared into one of the small offices off the lobby. Red stood up and walked over to her. "Finished giving Perkins all your vital information, Mama?" he asked.

She shook her cane at Red threateningly. "As a matter of fact, I didn't tell him everything. Although, after your reaction to it, I'm keeping my other news to myself." She started moving slowly towards the door, leaning on her cane as she walked.

"Now, that's a bad idea. For one thing, you shouldn't even *have* any news or information relating to this case. For another, if you do hear anything, you should immediately turn it over to the police. What have you heard?"

The urge to impress Red with her detecting abilities warred with the urge to keep all her findings secret to give herself an edge. The need to show off became too strong. "I just happened to be talking with Kitty Kirk at book club—."

"Because you're such a regular at book club, aren't you?" Red asked in a tight voice.

"Anyway, she said that she'd seen Benton Chambers at the church that morning. I think it was when she was pulling into the church parking for the Women of the Church meeting."

Red put a hand on her arm, stopping her slow progress out of the police station. "Mama, she was sure about that? She saw Benton Chambers at the church that morning?"

"Well, she saw a big-boned man with a cane. It must have been Benton."

"And she saw him *when* exactly?"

"Well, it must have been right before I got to the church and discovered the body. So he could have run in, bopped her on the head, and left really fast before I walked in and found the body. And Kitty went on over to the dining hall for the meeting."

"A figure. With big-bones and a cane. Right before you discovered the body." Red said.

Myrtle nodded.

Red hooted out loud. "Mama! Kitty Kirk is blind as a bat. And batty to boot. She saw *you*. Going into the church before you discovered Parke Stockard's body. *You* were the big-boned man with the cane!"

A red flush crept over Myrtle's face and she jerked open the heavy police station door, slamming it shut behind her on Red's raucous laughter. He opened the door back up and poked his head out. "Sorry, Mama. I shouldn't have laughed. Hey, if you want to go ahead and do your grocery shopping, I'll run you back home afterwards. Deal?"

Myrtle was divided between wanting to snub him and needing his help. She needed to get milk this trip and walking home with the gallon jug wasn't an option. "Okay," she said grudgingly.

"I'll give you a 25-minute head start before I come over. And I might need a couple of things there, too, so I'll go inside to meet up with you."

Red walked back into the station and Perkins said, "You're right, Red. She's nosing around. I did invite her to let me know if she remembered anything from the crime scene yesterday. But this was more like information she'd gotten by gossiping."

"She'll end up being the next victim. The murderer won't like all her snooping."

"Oh, I don't know if she'd end up being murdered, Red. But I *could* use your help on this case. You're totally distracted this morning, worrying about your mom." Red knew all the suspects personally and could be a real asset with his insights. That is, if Perkins could get his mind on the case.

"We need to find something for her to do," Perkins said. "It doesn't look like she's going to just give up. If we can give her a red herring to send her on a wild goose chase, then maybe we can give her a harmless direction for her investigation."

"I'll try anything at this point. I just can't understand why she's trying to take over my job."

"I don't think she's looking at it that way," answered Perkins slowly. "I think she wants to do something important. Something significant. Maybe something that will earn your respect and show everyone that she's not just some fluffy old lady."

"Or maybe the voices are telling her to do it," grumbled Red. Then he laughed. "No, she's not fluffy. If someone calls her 'sweetheart,' she'll snap their head off. But tell me more about your master plan to divert Mama down the bunny trail."

"If your mother could overhear us while we talked about an 'important lead,' we could give her a red herring. Somewhere safe, but out a little ways in the country. Got any ideas?"

Red puffed out his cheeks and thought for a minute. He laughed. "How about Crazy Dan's? He sells tires, boiled peanuts, and old car parts. He's out in the boondocks, too. We could get her out of the way for a while, then. It's hard to understand a word the guy says, too. Might even necessitate a return trip."

"How is she going to get out there, though? She doesn't have a car anymore, does she?"

Red smiled. "That's the beauty of the plan. She'd have to borrow a car from somebody...she does still have a license. That'll take up even more time."

"Is she still okay to drive?" asked Perkins with a little concern. "It sounds like it's been a while since she's been behind the wheel of a car."

"There again, it'll work out perfectly. She drives so slow that this will end up being a day trip," said Red.

"How are we going to let her overhear us?"

"Shouldn't be hard! She's gotten so obsessed with detective work, she's probably got the police station bugged." Red rubbed his eyes and said, "She's at the grocery store now and I'm supposed to pick her up there in a few minutes and run her back home. We could arrange a discussion over there within her earshot."

"She wouldn't find that suspicious?" asked Perkins.

"Ordinarily, she's sharp as a tack. But she's so caught up with detective work that she probably won't even see that we're laying a trap for her. She'll just be pleased as punch that she's got something to help her crack the case." Red glanced at his watch. "We'd better head over there. She's like clockwork with this errand and she's probably wrapping things up. We need to catch her before she gets to the checkout line."

MYRTLE'S CART WAS HALF-full as she frowned in concentration at the cereal selection. Where was the oatmeal? Just plain oatmeal? No wonder all the kids today couldn't sit still in classrooms. Forget ADHD, it was sugary cereal! Frosted Cocoa Crispy Puffs? Myrtle shook her head and rounded the aisle. She was horrified to see Erma Sherman in the produce section. She had just pulled a single banana off a bunch and was now working on removing a single strand of grapes from a large bunch. Myrtle backed up, looking for an escape route, but Erma had already spotted her. She charged up, pushing her buggy aggressively in front of her.

"Myrtle! Good to see you! Actually, it's good just to be out, considering I've been under the weather a little." Erma, relentless invader of personal space, maneuvered her cart alongside Myrtle's and peered curiously into her cart.

"Sorry to hear that, Erma. I hate to cut this short, but I don't want to keep you."

"Oh, you're not keeping me at all. I have lots of time right now," said Erma. "I was having these horrible pains. After I ate, mostly, but sometimes when I lay down."

Myrtle began to fervently wish Elaine had already bought her new cell phone for her. Cell phone rings nag you at the most *convenient* times sometimes.

"My dear mother, Lucia, had the same problem. And my mother's sister, too. My mother's sister had seven children. *Seven*! Can you believe it?" asked Erma.

Should she feign illness? No, Erma would probably follow her to the restroom, detailing more stomach and intestinal complaints.

"And my first cousin's child, well, she must be forty now. Imagine that. Forty! She called me the other day," continued Erma.

Myrtle startled at the abrupt bleating of a cell phone. Had a new phone teleported into her pocketbook from sheer longing? Then she saw Erma fumbling in her carry-on size pocketbook for her phone and Myrtle edged away from her. Myrtle gave a quick wave to the now-absorbed Erma. She wondered who would voluntarily sacrifice their morning for a conversation with Erma Sherman.

Myrtle decided to cut her losses and escape from the store while she still could. Besides, Red or Elaine would be by soon to drive her and her groceries home. Their lives were all bound in these little routines that rarely changed. Myrtle walked to the store in good weather at 9:30 every Wednesday. Red or Elaine picked her up at 10:15 and drove her home. Her watch told her it was slightly past time—no surprise, considering Erma's determination to detail her deteriorating health.

Red and Lieutenant Perkins had already established themselves in the condiments aisle and watched Myrtle hurry in their direction toward the checkout line. Red started talking loudly and Myrtle stopped, creeping closer to the end of the aisle.

"Perkins, you find that creamer you wanted for the coffee maker at the station? Mama should be about ready to go. We're going to interview that possible informant?"

"Yes, let's get some questions ready when we get back to the station. But I don't think we'll get around to visiting him today; it'll probably be tomorrow. What was this fellow's name again?"

"Crazy Dan. He runs the hubcap and peanut stand out that rural route," Red helpfully pointed out.

"Right. It really sounds like he might have some important information. Well, let's find your mother and go check out."

Flustered, Myrtle whipped the cart around, only to see Erma Sherman wrapping up her cell phone conversation. In a panic now, she hurried toward the back of the store and the meat counter to approach Red and Perkins from the back. Crazy Dan? What on earth could he contribute to a murder investigation? At least she'd gotten a tip from them, finally. She greeted the two men distractedly, not noticing them wink at each other.

Myrtle was so preoccupied on the drive home, it barely registered when Red handed her the new cell phone that Elaine had picked up for her. But she did notice that Red seemed a little grumpier than usual, and it couldn't be just because of her. She offered up a couple of chatty lines of conversation, only to have them greeted with grunts. Finally, Red spoke his mind. "Mama, I have an awful feeling you want to get involved in this murder investigation. It sure looked like you'd been nosing around the crime scene."

"As I told you, I just made sure Parke didn't need medical treatment. It seems to me, though, that you'd be interested in hearing my ideas on the murder."

Red said, "You shouldn't be having any ideas! You should just be sitting on your screened porch with a good book, or watching soap operas and fussing over the crazy story lines." His voice grew softer. "You've had great ideas your whole life. Why not just chill out for a while? You could be like Nero Wolfe and mull the case while you harvest your backyard tomatoes. Then you can share your insights with me."

When Myrtle didn't budge, he sighed. Besides," he added grimly, "I've got my hands full enough as it is. Between a murder investigation and hosting a French exchange student, life is out of control."

Myrtle shifted uneasily and fiddled with the seat belt. She was the one who'd suggested that they host the exchange student. Months ago, Myrtle witnessed Elaine's uncharacteristic meltdown directly following a powerful toddler tantrum. "I'm not just a bottom-swabber....a boo-boo kisser, you know," she'd fumed.

Myrtle had gotten distracted, as usual. "Excellent use of kennings, Elaine. Very clever."

"What?"

"Kennings, Elaine. You remember...the Anglo-Saxon poetry device...you know...whale's way?" Elaine looked blank. "Another way of saying 'the sea?' From *Beowulf*?"

"Going back to my rant..."

"Sorry, Elaine. You're right, of course. You're much more than that."

"Anyway, you've effectively illustrated that I've forgotten 90% of everything I learned in school. I don't remember basic French, Myrtle. I can't even conjugate a verb! And I was a French major," said Elaine.

She'd sounded so dejected that Myrtle dreamed up the idea of Red and Elaine hosting a French exchange student. It would give her a chance to practice French and experience another world without leaving her home and her mothering duties. And it had seemed to have helped Elaine at first. She'd at least seemed happy, despite spewing out miserably unintelligible French at the poor student.

"How *is* Jean-Marc?" Myrtle delicately asked Red.

Red snorted. "Jean-Marc is just fine, but every appliance in our house is on the blink. He tinkers with everything and everything he touches bites the dust. Our house is an appliance graveyard."

Myrtle snickered and Red said, "Don't think it's so funny, Mama. He wants to pilot the boat next."

"Well, it's not my boat anymore. It's yours. It just happens to be docked at my house, that's all."

"You won't feel that way when he plows that boat through the dock and up into your yard."

"There you go—exaggerating again, Red. He's doing Elaine a world of good, mark my words. She was stuck in a rut. 'The problem that has no name,' or whatever. Now she's speaking French, and feeling connected to the wide, wonderful world out there."

"I know a smattering of French, Mama, and I don't think that's what Elaine is speaking. Jean-Marc pounds his head when she talks to him."

"She'll improve with practice, Red."

He shrugged and Myrtle said, "She was in this domestic funk. It's hard you know—white loads and dark loads and ring around the collar. Wiping off sticky baby faces. She wanted a chance to exercise her brain."

Just like me, thought Myrtle glumly.

"Therapy would have been cheaper. We'll be up to our necks wading around in broken DVD players, lawnmowers, cars, and boats. I can't wait to ship him back to France." A disbelieving note crept into his voice. "He was swigging a glass of my chardonnay in the kitchen the other night!"

"Well, he's sixteen after all."

"Drinking age is twenty-one, Mama."

"Not in France, it's not. He's probably used to drinking a glass of wine with dinner."

"I'm the police chief. I can't be aiding and abetting an underage drinker in my own house!"

"But Elaine is polishing her French and expanding her world view. He's *good* for her."

"Funny that what's good for Elaine is so rotten for me," he responded glumly.

As soon as Red dropped her off at the house and carried her groceries in, she tried to organize her thoughts. Who would she borrow the car from? She still had her driver's license, with the new 15-year expiration date to cover her until her century-mark. But she'd given up driving awhile back and had sold her car long ago. Elaine need her van to transport Jack in a carrier. Erma Sherman? She shuddered. Erma had actually offered her car to Myrtle before, but would she insist on going along and helping her on whatever "errand" Myrtle cooked up?

Germs. That was a common thread in many of Erma's monologues. She loved to talk about her health problems, but was a germaphobe. That could be her ticket to ride. She picked up the phone.

"Erma? Hi, it's Myrtle. You know, after I saw you at the grocery store, I just started feeling *awful*. No, nothing like that, just this stomach and intestinal thing. I was wondering if I could use your car for a little while this afternoon and go to the doctor. I'd ask Red or Elaine, but they're so busy today. No, ordinarily it would be great if you took me, but I'm afraid I'd give this to you...and it's *really awful*. I feel wretched. Oh, thanks, Erma. I'll be right outside."

Myrtle heard a crash and looked out her window. A squirrel sat on his haunches on her birdfeeder, casually munching the peanuts she'd put out for the bluebirds. Myrtle banged on the window with her fist and the squirrel turned its head, eyeing her curiously as it ate. She yanked open the back door and waved her cane at it and it finally scurried off into Erma's yard. Typical. Erma had established a sanctuary for the little rodents, stocked with nuts, corn, water, and building supplies for their ratty-looking nests. She went to the Piggly-Wiggly once a week for more food for her feral flock. Anybody who fed squirrels on purpose had to be squirrelly too. The squirrel sat at the edge of Myrtle's yard, watching the back door. As soon as she was gone, it was going to hop back up and finish its lunch.

Myrtle thumped her way through the house and out the front door. Erma was already outside, holding a plastic bag and her car keys. One squirrel was a foot behind her in the driveway, and she clucked to it and tossed it some peanuts. Another perched on the top of her old Cadillac like a furry hood ornament.

She wiped off some of her makeup and mussed her hair a little and stepped outside. She must have done a good job. Erma stayed back and reached her arm way out to hand Myrtle the keys. "You look *awful*. Do you think you need to upchuck?" She peered anxiously into Myrtle's face and Myrtle thought she might have to after all. "You're looking kind of green. Here's a bag in case you need to throw up in the car. Good luck at the doctor." She paused and looked at Myrtle uncertainly. "Have you...um...driven recently?"

"Certainly. Five years ago."

"That's *recent*?"

"Time is relative when you're my age. Don't worry—I've always been an excellent driver."

Erma crooned to the squirrelly hood ornament and it hopped off the car and up the driveway. It crossed over into Myrtle's yard and she put her hand on the horn to honk, but thought twice about it. She was supposed to be at death's door, so probably shouldn't seem too concerned about rodent eating habits.

If Erma had envisioned Myrtle peeling rubber as she raced off to the doctor, she was quickly relieved when she carefully pulled the stick into reverse, looked thoroughly behind her as she backed up, and drove off down the street at a sedate 20 miles an hour.

Chapter Five

Crazy Dan's little piece of the world was located out on the rural route highway that had been a major thoroughfare before the advent of the interstate system. The rural route was dotted by deserted roadside motels, old farms with some dwarfed cotton stalks that looked like dried-up sticks, and bait shops with beer signs in the windows.

The number of Jesus signs increased in proportion to the distance from Bradley. They started out "Jesus Saves" and got less-comforting as she drove on out. By the time Myrtle was out in the sticks, the signs warned her of the imminent loss of her soul. She passed little bitty houses with big satellite dishes on the roof and an expensive pick-up in the driveway. A series of rotting wooden signs proclaimed "CRAZY Dan's Boil P-Nuts, Hubcaps, Fireworks (Fireworks was long-since crossed off, due to state law), Live Bait!" Next to it was a weather-beaten sign that looked like a palm with "Madam Zora, psychic" written on it. Actually, it had "sykick" on it, but Myrtle deciphered the meaning. Apparently, Madam Zora also read "tarro cards."

"One stop shopping," muttered Myrtle as she pulled Erma's car off the street and onto a barren stretch of red clay that Myrtle guessed was the parking lot. Most of the yard looked that way, though. The house was the most startling thing on the lot. At least, Myrtle guessed there was a house lurking underneath the hubcaps. Everything from the roof down was completely covered with every type of hubcap imaginable. Only a couple of dirty windows remained uncovered. She sat in the car and just stared at it. What did it sound like during a rainstorm? Who would do something like this? The kind of person who would have information about a murder, she decided. She grabbed her cane from the passenger's seat and opened the car door.

Since no one had come out, she made her way up to the front door of the hubcap house. She could see no discernible doorbell and the door was completely covered by hubcaps. How was she supposed to let him know she was there? She rapped at a hubcap with her cane, which made a metallic reverberating sound, and she was rewarded by an opening door. Staring at her was a grizzly little man with bony features, leathery skin, mangy-looking stubble, and nicotine-stained hands. He glared at her. "Whatcha want?"

Some salesman. "What if I told you I wanted boiled peanuts or hubcaps? Aren't you in business to sell things to people?"

He grunted. "Ain't got no boil peanuts. You want hubcaps, jest looka th' house." He started to close the door and Myrtle stuck her cane in the doorway. He raised wispy eyebrows and said, "Whatchadoin'? You crazy?"

"No, but *you* are. They call you Crazy Dan for *some* reason. I need to talk to you for a minute." When he motioned her into his shadowy and rather rank-smelling house, she added, "Outside will be fine."

Outside really *wasn't* fine. It was probably over 100 degrees, although Myrtle had a feeling Crazy Dan's house wasn't much better. She saw a decrepit window unit sagging out of one window, propped up by a couple of hubcaps. The unit made a sluggish, chugging sound, then stopped abruptly. Crazy Dan reached out and slapped the back of it, spawning it into a lethargic-sounding drone. How he lived in the South in a home that resembled a giant sun-catcher without central air, Myrtle couldn't figure. Crazy Dan's mutts lay in shadows of bushes, trees, and the house, apparently only moving when the shadow moved or to wet their whistles in their water bowls.

He was working on a huge wad of chewing tobacco, which had apparently just gotten to the right point to spit out. Squinting over at a spot, he spat out a stream of the brown juice to splatter in the red dust.

Myrtle was starting to feel as though she'd walked through the looking glass. She knew there was information to be had, but couldn't figure out for the life of her what Crazy Dan could possibly know. About anything.

She decided that the direct approach would work best. "Do you know anything about the murder of Parke Stockard?" Crazy Dan's leathery face wrinkled even more than it already was. He seemed to be in danger of losing his features altogether in the folds of skin.

"Parke Stock-kard?" he rolled the name around on his tongue as if trying out an exotic dish that wasn't very pleasing to him. He was thoughtful. "That Yankee, weren't she?"

Former-English-teacher Myrtle repressed a sigh. "That's right."

He thought for a moment and Myrtle wondered if this was the first time his mind had been exercised in a while. She could almost hear the squeaks from the rusty cerebral equipment. He opened his mouth wide and Myrtle leaned in, sure to finally hear the valuable recollection that had prompted this visit.

Crazy Dan burped.

Myrtle turned around and started maneuvering her way around piles of hubcaps towards Erma's car. "I suppose that's a no, Mr. Dan," she called back over her shoulder. She stumbled over an exposed tree root, sticking up out of the red clay of his yard and would have fallen if Crazy Dan hadn't caught her with one sweep of his surprisingly wiry arm.

She turned to thank him for his gallantry, but stopped at his scowl. "Don't be fallin' down in *my* yard. Suin' me, mos' like."

For reparations in hubcaps and boil p-nuts, guessed Myrtle. She yanked herself out of his grasp. "Sorry for the imposition, Crazy. I mean, Mr. Dan. Someone mentioned that you knew something. Obviously, an incorrect assumption in every respect."

Crazy Dan wheezed out a laugh. "Well, tha' might be and mightn't be."

Had she fallen down the rabbit hole? Crazy Dan was starting to take an amazing resemblance to the Mad Hatter. "Or maybe the Dormouse?" she mused aloud. "No, that was the one that was always falling asleep. The March Hare!"

Crazy Dan squinted at her suspiciously, perhaps thinking she should adopt the name Mad Myrtle then said cautiously, "Dunno 'bout that, though. But I see things. Livin' in the country, y'see things."

Myrtle bit back a tart response and sweetly asked, "What things, Mr. Dan?"

"Seen tha' politician with the hussy. Lotsa times. Thinks his runnin' around is safe out in the backwoods. Thinks I don't know whose BM-dubyer it is!" He snorted in continued disbelief.

Myrtle stared into Crazy Dan's creased face. "That is kind of weird that he would feel anonymous. Considering cars are your specialty, judging from the number in your yard. So it was definitely a BMW and you're sure it was Benton Chambers with this hussy?"

"I'm sure it was his *BM-dubyer.*"

Myrtle held out her hand to Crazy Dan, who shook it with a suntanned paw. "Thank you, Mr. Dan. You've been very helpful."

He held onto Myrtle's hand for a second, looking at it thoughtfully, then glancing at Myrtle's large pocketbook. He grunted. "You oughta be talkin' to muh sister. Wander."

"Your sister wanders?" He was losing Myrtle again.

Crazy Dan looked at Myrtle with the same expression he might give a splinter stuck in his brown paw. "Naw! Her *name* is Wander."

Must be the psychic with the giant palm next to Crazy Dan's sign. She started to stop him when he suddenly started yelling, "Wander! Wander! C'mere! You got a palm to read."

Out came a woman who Myrtle would have thought was Crazy Dan in drag if Dan hadn't still been standing in front of her. She looked nothing like the mystic-sounding name "Madam Zora" would have you believe. The skin-and-bones creature flashed a smile with five or six teeth missing and said hoarsely, "Lemme see yer palm."

Crazy Dan nodded and looked at Myrtle expectantly, so Myrtle surrendered her hand to the woman. Wanda held it with nicotine-stained hands and looked searchingly at her palm before dropping it as if it was on fire and turning around to go back in the hubcap-covered hut. "Hey!" bellowed Crazy Dan. "What about th' money? Give 'er th' for-toon, Wander!"

But Wanda waved him away with a flap of her hand. She paused in the doorway before entering the dark interior of the house and called out in a cigarette-damaged croak, "Stop everything. You're in bad danger." As quickly as she'd appeared, she vanished.

Chapter Six

I n danger. The psychic's eerie prediction—more like a pronouncement—bothered Myrtle during the long drive back. Wanda had seemed genuinely shaken and had refused to take her money, which hadn't endeared her to Crazy Dan. But the woman couldn't actually be clairvoyant. It was more likely that she was completely off her rocker. Who *wouldn't* be, living with Crazy Dan?

Myrtle did remember to put some gas into Erma's tank, in case she wondered why going to the doctor would put such a dent in her tank. She pulled into a station and scrounged a couple of dollars from her pocketbook. Then she saw how far two dollars would go and nearly keeled over from the sticker shock. Five years without a car and the price of gas had skyrocketed. She dug out more money.

Myrtle pulled cautiously up into Erma's driveway, hoping to limit the interaction with her. No problems there. Erma apparently had no desire to catch any stomach or intestinal bugs.

"Hope you feel better, Myrtle," she said briskly, spraying the car keys with an industrial-sized can of Lysol when Myrtle handed them to her. The last Myrtle saw of her, she was lost in an anti-bacterial cloud as she sprayed down the entire interior of her car.

Myrtle spent several hours that night studying the ceiling crack. The entire encounter put a very bad taste in Myrtle's mouth. The next morning, she walked downtown to Bo's Diner for one of their pimento cheese slaw dog and chili fries plates. Nothing was very worrisome when you had a greasy plate of food in front of you.

Bo's Diner in downtown Bradley was *the* place to go for lunch and had been for forty years, when Bo's father owned it. Plus, it had the best sweet tea in the South. A bell jangled when she opened the door and Bo looked up from behind the counter and greeted her. The diner had frayed vinyl booths around Formica-topped tables. A sign on the wall stated: "If You Can't Say it in Front of Granny, Don't Say it Here!" There was nothing new about the place, but everything was kept immaculately clean.

Myrtle slid into a high-backed vinyl booth and a waitress with "Tanya" on her nametag approached with an order pad. Myrtle winced. Tanya was fond of treating her like a particularly slow toddler. "Hey there, sweetheart! Was your little tummy rumbling for something yummy? Glad you came in to visit ole Tanya, sweetie. What can I get for your rumbly tummy?"

Soppy condescension was a big reason Myrtle hated being old. She'd never have tolerated that kind of disrespect all those years in her classroom. She bet itsy bitsy Tanya wouldn't be smiling when her tip was reduced. Or when Myrtle solved the murder everybody in town was talking about.

Myrtle's favorite waitress noticed Myrtle's disgusted expression and quickly intervened. Shelia wasn't sure if she was saving Myrtle from Tanya's sugary sweetness, or Tanya from a blistering reply.

"Hey, Tanya. It's time for your break, isn't it? I'll take your tables."

Tanya's mouth opened and she closed it back up again. "Already? Well, I could use a smoke. See you later, lovey," she said to Myrtle with a smile. Myrtle bared her teeth in return.

"My hero," said Myrtle. Shelia's grin brightened her still-pretty middle-aged face.

"Don't mention it. It's slow now, anyway. Tanya *was* due for a break. Although it's a little early for it." And Shelia smiled again.

Ten minutes later, a greasy plate heaped with chili fries and the hot dog arrived at the table and Shelia plopped down in the booth across from Myrtle. "If you've got a second to chat, I'll get off my feet for a minute."

Myrtle looked as innocuously gossip-craven as she could. "Now that you're here, you can give me a little insider gossip. No, don't give me that innocent look. You know you've got your finger on the town pulse. Got any ideas about who killed Parke Stockard?"

The waitress laughed, "I should be asking you. You discovered her body."

Myrtle impatiently waved a blue-veined hand around in the air. "That wasn't anything. What I'm interested in hearing is who had a beef with Parke." She took a healthy bite of her hot dog.

"Well, that would be half the town, Miss Myrtle. Pretty as she was, she wasn't going to win any popularity contests around here."

"Because people were jealous of her? For being rich and beautiful?"

"Being rich and beautiful was okay, but being pushy and mean wasn't. One of our customers here used to live on Boulevard in one of those real fancy houses... about sixty years old, beautiful architecture. I'm not saying she's unhappy about all the money she made from selling the land to Parke. But Parke was a total witch when she pressured her to sell. She kept harping on the old, crummy kitchen and outdated décor. She convinced her she could never sell it with the new homes competing for buyers right down the street. It was just her tone of voice and the way she'd flip her hair out of her face and roll her eyes. She was cocky." Shelia shook her head. "No one could stand her."

"And this kind of pressure is what Parke tried to apply to Tanner and Althea Hayes, right?" asked Myrtle, before taking a big sip from her sweet tea.

Shelia nodded. "Yes ma'am. That's what I hear, anyway. I heard Althea talk to her nephew Josh—the newspaper guy—about it. She said Tanner was determined not to sell their land to Parke's development company. But Parke was just as determined to get it. She said some really ugly things to him right before he had a massive heart attack and died out in their front yard. Poor Althea. She seems lost without him."

"Who else was upset with Parke?"

The waitress blew out a gusty sigh and tapped her fake fingernails on the Formica-topped table. "Who wasn't?"

"Well, I know about the Benton Chambers conflict, of course. That's public knowledge."

Shelia raised carefully plucked brows. "Their affair was public knowledge?"

"What? No, I meant that she was trying to pressure him into being friendlier to development and zoning changes. What affair?"

Shelia picked up a fork and flipped it over and over thoughtfully. "I guess that *might* have been a way to pressure Benton. I sure can't see any other reason for her to get involved with him. Parke was gorgeous and could have had any man in town eating out of her hand. And Benton?" Shelia made a face.

Myrtle said, "He was much better looking when he was a younger man."

She squinted doubtfully. "If you say so, Miss Myrtle. But he's nobody's pretty child now."

"Back to this affair, though. *You* know about it, so it obviously couldn't have been all *that* secret?"

Shelia shook her head a quick no, ponytail swishing from side to side. "No, I think it *was* a secret. I just happened to overhear Parke when she was waiting to pay for lunch at the counter and talking to Benton."

"What was she saying to him?"

"Parke was talking in this really tight voice. Saying something about her thinking the time they shared together might have made him realize how important the development project on Boulevard was to her. Benton was just babbling away, not really saying anything."

Myrtle said mildly, "But she could have been talking about a meeting they'd had in his office where she'd explained her position on the development plan."

Shelia gave a wheezy laugh. "If they had a meeting in his office, it was a closed-door one. Parke's voice got real ugly. She said she'd never have wasted her time on him if she hadn't thought he'd change his mind about rezoning Boulevard. Then...." Shelia pinched her frosted pink mouth shut.

Myrtle prompted, "Well?"

"Well, I couldn't hear the next part as well. But it sounded like she was threatening him."

"As if she'd tell everyone about their affair if he didn't change his position and support development?"

The waitress shook her head vigorously. "No. Like she'd tell about a *different* affair that she knew about."

This might be the one Crazy Dan knew about. Unless there was yet another one. "When does Benton have time to work on Bradley's business?"

"I don't know, Miss Myrtle. But it makes sense that Parke wouldn't want to tell about *their* affair. She'd have ended up looking about as bad as he would if word got out. And she was trying to sell people on her company."

The bells on the diner door rang out as Josh Tucker walked in. Shelia nodded towards him. "And that one wasn't happy with Miss Priss, either. Not one bit."

"Josh Tucker? Why on earth would he be upset with Parke?"

Shelia leaned towards Myrtle and folded and refolded a napkin, making a careful crease. "He was telling Althea—his aunt, you know—something about Parke. I couldn't hear all of it, but he was mad. Then the next day, he was almost yelling at Sloan Jones for cutting one of his articles to make more room for Parke's piece. It didn't sound like the first time they'd argued about it, either."

Myrtle sat back with a whump into the vinyl backed booth. "I had no idea. I mean, I knew Sloan was cutting *my* stuff, but to cut Wonder Boy's pieces is really something." She drank more sweet tea. "So he must have been telling Althea how frustrated he was, too."

"Well, he has ended up being kind of a big shot in the town. Winning that award for the *Bugle* and everything."

Myrtle looked cross at the reminder.

"Plus the fact that Josh is real close to his aunt and uncle, you know. I bet he didn't take kindly to the fact that Parke Stockard killed his uncle."

Myrtle choked a little on the last of her chili fries. "Is that what people are saying? That Parke killed Tanner?"

"She might just as well have picked up a gun and shot him, Miss Myrtle; the outcome was the same. She got him all fired up and next thing you know he was a goner with a heart attack. Too much Parke Stockard."

More likely too many hot dogs and chili fries at Bo's Diner. Myrtle looked at her empty plate ruefully. Tanner was a regular for lunch, and it probably caught up with his arteries.

Bo called out to Shelia, "Hey, we've got two orders up!"

Shelia stood up, fished the check out of her apron pocket and handed it to Myrtle to take up front. "I've got to run, Miss Myrtle. Good talking with you."

Myrtle saw Tanya coming back out and hustled to the cash register. "You take care, sweet-ums!" she hollered across the diner.

"You too, sugar pops!" returned Myrtle, as she fished some cash out of her pocketbook.

Chapter Seven

The diner door swung shut behind her as Myrtle started walking home. It was one of those hot afternoons where the breeze made you hotter instead of cooling you off. She was full of greasy food and taking a nap during her favorite soap opera, *Tomorrow's Promise*, was the next order of business.

Her plans were foiled, however, with a yoo-hoo from behind her. Myrtle's face was pained as Erma Sherman drove up and pulled over onto the curb. She opened the car door and waddled towards Myrtle. She was wearing a large-print, flowered dress that hung on her big frame like a tent.

Myrtle flinched as Erma sidled up into her personal space to talk. Her large, rodent-like teeth were exposed in what Erma fondly thought of as a smile. "Where are you heading, Myrtle? I'll drive you there. You shouldn't be walking to the store like this—you were at death's door yesterday and you don't look a bit better today."

"Thanks," mumbled Myrtle. There was no point arguing that she hadn't been going to the store or that she felt perfectly fine. Erma Sherman was an unstoppable force of nature.

Erma completely ignored Myrtle's weak refusal as she bull-dozed her towards her elderly Cadillac. The inside of the car reeked of menthol cough drops. As they drove off, Erma provided a running commentary about the trouble her bunions were giving her. She was either going deaf or was determined to hold onto her captive audience. They drove by Myrtle's house and Myrtle pounded on the car window, pointing helplessly as Erma's tale of podiatric woe continued. Finally, Myrtle gave in to her misery, slumping in the seat. The amount of nonsense spewing out of Erma's mouth was amazing. Without listening to Erma's monologue, Myrtle watched her face. She half expected whiskers to sprout on either side of her long nose. She really *did* look like a rat.

"...especially since Kitty *poisoned* Parke. Because that was no accident. But you know, I've never liked Kitty's casseroles. *Especially* her chicken a la king. So I had to agree with Parke there. My stomach problems, you know. The other day I was eating tuna...."

"Whoa!" said Myrtle. And Erma reigned in with surprise. "What are you talking about? Kitty poisoning Parke Stockard? What?"

Erma looked nonplussed. "Well, Wednesday night fellowship a few weeks ago. Parke had been complaining for months about Kitty's 'uninspired casseroles.' And everybody knew Parke was allergic to shellfish. Kitty, of *all* people, knew that. She's been so careful about the flower arrangements for altar guild, you know—no roses. Because that *wonderful* reporter at the *Bugle*—Josh Tucker? He's horribly allergic to roses. So she always brings wildflowers—"

"The *poisoning*?" gritted Myrtle between her teeth, cutting off another Erma Sherman homage to Josh Tucker.

"So she would have been careful not to have any shellfish at the Wednesday night dinners. Because she makes notes about things like that. Besides, the church budget is a chicken budget, not a seafood budget."

Myrtle gave an exasperated sigh.

"But she *did*—she put crabmeat in a casserole and told everyone it was "chicken surprise." Erma gave a squeaky laugh. "It was a surprise, all right. Parke swelled up, broke out in a rash, had trouble breathing. They took her to the hospital. Did I tell you about the last time I went to the hospital? I had this kidney stone."

Myrtle tuned back out. Was Kitty worried because the police might want to question her over the food poisoning a few weeks ago? Or was she worried because she had lashed out at Parke Stockard again, this time killing her?

"Anyway, I'm glad to see you're all right before I go out of town for the next couple of days." She paused, a cue for Myrtle to ask where she was going. Myrtle didn't comply.

"I'm going to the casino. The one on the reservation? You need to go with me some time. Sometimes I come back with ever so much money. But then, I've always had good luck."

Myrtle doubted that very much. Erma certainly hadn't won the looks lottery. Finally able to get a word in, she said, "I don't gamble though, Erma. So I won't be interested."

Erma said, "But you'd have fun. The old folks' bus takes us. The senior recreation program. Besides, lots of people gamble, Myrtle. You'd be surprised."

Myrtle's look said that she *would* be surprised, and Erma said, "Even the rich folks gamble, Myrtle. I've seen Cecil Stockard there many times." Noticing she'd finally gotten Myrtle's attention, Erma added importantly, "And he's a big roller. You know about those?"

"Yes, I know what a big roller is," said Myrtle impatiently.

"You're sure about that?"

"Of course, I am. I even hear that he gambles on the Internet, too. I wonder if he's won a ton of money."

Or lost a ton of money. That could provide a motive for murder.

Myrtle jolted back to the present when Erma ran over a curb, coasted diagonally into a parking place and slammed on her brakes.

"Well, here we are. I'll see you later." Myrtle was about to open her mouth to protest when the driver's door slammed. As abruptly as she'd appeared, Erma disappeared, barreling through the "exit" door of the grocery store.

Stunned, Myrtle sat in Erma's car for a couple of minutes before fishing in her pocketbook for her cell phone.

"Elaine? Thank God you're there! Can you run by the grocery store and pick me up? I was hijacked by Erma Sherman. I was planning on walking back home, but that woman sapped all the energy out of me. You don't need anything from the store, do you? No? Yes, five minutes would be great."

Myrtle pulled herself out of the old Cadillac—which wasn't easy since she was practically sitting on the pavement in the car. She slammed the door in irritation behind her. She walked to the front of the grocery store and leaned against the wall to wait for Elaine.

The day was a real scorcher with steam rising off the parking lot pavement and Myrtle, wishing she could perspire better than she did and cool off a little. It was the kind of day where the ice cream truck trolled the streets for hot, thirsty kids. And the kind of day where the kids' ice cream immediately melted on impact with the humid wall of air.

A Mercedes sped into the parking lot and Benton Chambers, the councilman, jumped out. *Jumped* out might be an exaggeration, since he was carrying a cane and had a large cast on his right leg. Myrtle squinted at him. He seemed to be talking to himself in a very animated fashion. Then she noticed a cell phone attachment clipped to his ear.

He talked on his phone as he hobbled past Myrtle. She sniffed. She was sure *she* hadn't been yelling when she'd called Elaine. She couldn't stand people who bellowed into their phones. Myrtle's phone was just a couple of years old but already looked as if it hailed from prehistoric man. She'd asked Red just the other day to shop for a new phone for her since the battery on her old one wasn't holding its charge well anymore.

"I'm right on it, Don. Yes, the file is on my desk and I'm looking at it as we speak." Benton met Myrtle's startled gaze and winked at her. She supposed politicians spent a majority of their time fibbing.

Elaine's green minivan pulled into a space and Myrtle climbed into the front seat. Elaine looked frazzled. Her normally sleek bob stuck up in places where she must have run her fingers through it. Jean-Marc, the exchange student, was smirking in the backseat. "Accidentally broke the coffee maker," murmured Elaine. No more explanation was necessary. Myrtle could envision a morning in the Clover house without an immediate caffeine infusion. Red without java? It wouldn't have been a pretty picture.

Myrtle turned a suspicious eye at the backseat (she was convinced Jean-Marc knew more English than he was letting on) and then told Elaine about getting hijacked by Erma Sherman and the conversation—actually, a monologue—that followed. But she wasn't sure Elaine was really listening. Jean-Marc was paying more attention in the back of the car. He gave a nod when she looked back at him again. "Erma Sherman," he repeated. Then he pantomimed something that looked like a giant rodent. He looked questioningly at Myrtle and she nodded in affirmation. That was Erma all right. Jack giggled and made a rat-face, too.

"By the way, thanks for picking up the new phone for me, Elaine."

"Hmm? Oh. Yes, it had all the bells and whistles."

Exactly what Myrtle didn't like about it. But she guessed that you couldn't find just a regular phone anymore. Now if she could only figure out how to make the thing stop playing the "Star Spangled Banner" when it rang.

Elaine realized that Myrtle was waiting for her to do or say something. They had pulled into Myrtle's driveway and she suddenly noticed Myrtle wasn't opening the door to get out and seemed to be waiting for her to say something in response. "Um...yes, poor Erma. Those bunions can be awful. Well, I'm off to get another coffee maker. You'll be okay to walk home from here?"

Myrtle slowly opened the minivan door and stepped out. So there would be no crime-fighting duo—Elaine had too much going on. She was on her own.

Chapter Eight

Later, Myrtle and Elaine squeezed into a packed pew in the packed sanctuary of the church for Parke's funeral. "Too bad we couldn't get better seats," Myrtle muttered, pulling her glasses out of her pocketbook, and closing the purse with a snap.

"Well, it's not a play. We should be able to follow what's going on from back here."

"Not a play, but maybe a circus. Is that a brass section in front of the choir loft? What's this thing they handed us?" demanded Myrtle.

Red plopped on the pew between them and put his arms around them because there wasn't enough room for his arms next to him in the pew. "These things are programs, Mama." He chuckled at the stricken expression on Myrtle's face. "Apparently we're going to be treated to most of Handel's "Messiah" while we're here."

Myrtle pulled up on the pew in front of her and squinted to prove to herself that there was indeed a brass section next to the full choir in the loft. She plopped back into the pew, wincing at the hardness of the wooden pews. "You'd think if Parke Stockard were so keen on updating the church that she'd have pitched in for some pew cushions." Red raised his eyebrows. "You know," said Myrtle, waving her hands around. "You'd have thought she'd have wanted to add red pew cushions as a nice complement to the sanctuary's furnishings. Considering how much she liked to show off, too."

"She was a real Philistine," drawled Red, rolling his eyes.

Elaine tried ignoring their exchange, taking a deep breath and letting the beauty of the church relax her. The smooth, hand-carved wooden pews gleamed with polish. Although the pews seated 350, the way the pews curved around in semi-circles on each side towards the altar gave the sanctuary a more intimate feel. Corinthian columns held up a vaulted ceiling and large, leaded, stained glass windows featuring elaborate depictions of Biblical stories lined the walls. The church dated back to the late-1800s and functioned not only as a church, but also as a host for different community events.

The brass ensemble suddenly trumpeted and Myrtle leapt off the pew. To cover her confusion, she picked up a hymnbook from the rack in front of her. She flipped idly through its new pages, then peered at the composers and hymn titles in dismay.

Elaine leaned over and bellowed into Myrtle's ear to compete with the music. "What's wrong? You have a horrible expression on your face."

"I'm at a funeral after all," said Myrtle crossly. She pointed at a hymn and thumped the page. "These new hymnbooks have only modern music in them. Nothing written before 1975!" She flipped to the front cover of the hymnal. "Ah. "Donated to the Glory of God through Parke Stockard." Myrtle frowned. "That's worded oddly. Like she thought she was God's conduit or something."

The horns swelled, then mercifully quieted while the choir sang a quieter selection. Elaine whispered, "Well, there's been a lot of disagreement with the changes that Parke Stockard has implemented in the church since her arrival." Myrtle looked surprised and Elaine coughed. "You—haven't attended church for a while."

"All right. Point taken. What other changes has she made?"

"Modernized the service. She paid for so much that I don't think Nathaniel Gluck could tell her no. Brought in huge flower arrangements for the altar. New robes for the choir and minister. Spruced up the sanctuary. Hired special musicians to come in and play—not always the most formal music either," said Elaine.

"Really?" Myrtle asked dubiously as Handel's Messiah reached another fever pitch in front of them.

"Sometimes really contemporary stuff. Made a lot of the old fogies in the congregation upset, but what could the preacher do? She was paying for it all."

Myrtle opened her mouth again but stopped short when Erma Sherman glared at her, pointing dramatically to the open casket before assuming a pious pose. Elaine hid her giggles by coughing as Myrtle grouchily snatched up her program to see how much progress they'd made. She made a mental note to brave Kitty Kirk's house and ask her about the changes to the church service. She'd be amazed if Kitty had an understanding, Christian attitude about the changes. Myrtle peered around the sanctuary until she spotted Kitty. She sat near the front, wearing a respectful black dress and she actually appeared somewhat pulled together. Her hair was up in a nondescript bun and she wore a faint smile on her face. Thanking God for her blessings?

Nathaniel Gluck was now delivering some sort of homily. Myrtle groaned loudly enough for Elaine to shake her head. But a minute later she sat up to attention. Parke's daughter, right off a plane from New York, approached the microphone and introduced herself as Cecilia. Cecil, dragging his feet a bit, followed at a distance behind her. Myrtle watched Cecil with dislike. He had the carefully cultivated look of a complete degenerate. His black hair was thick with oily gel, making him look as slick as he sounded. He was handsome in a smarmy kind of way, with big, white, perfect teeth that had the unfortunate habit of flashing when he smirked, which was frequently. His clothes were flashy, as if a pimp were his principal fashion influence.

Myrtle leaned over and stage-whispered at Red, "Parke Stockard was obviously deranged. Who names their children Cecil and Cecilia?"

Red ignored her.

Parke's daughter cleared her throat. Looking out over the packed sanctuary, Cecilia cleared her throat again. She was dressed in an expensive-looking navy suit and wore many large diamond rings. She twisted one of them around on her finger and hesitated. The sanctuary waited with bated breath for whatever words of wisdom Cecilia was going to offer. They were doubtlessly hoping for some sort of clue as to the killer. *This* was the moment they'd waited for, the reason for attending. No Handel for this crowd—they wanted dirty laundry.

Parke's daughter paused again. She seemed to be searching the recesses of her brain for something to say. She looked at Cecil, who shrugged. Finally, she dredged up a deep breath and said, "Mother would have loved the service. Thanks so much for coming." And she scurried back to her pew, high heels clicking on the hardwood before she reached the thick red carpeting. Cecil smirked as he trailed behind her.

The sanctuary sighed with collective disappointment. There was a rustling of programs as if everyone was checking to see if the service was nearly over. It was, after the grand finale of the Hallelujah chorus, which everyone in the congregation stood respectfully for. Myrtle caught the florist looking heavenward as if echoing the words. Myrtle looked around for anyone else looking especially smug. The Hallelujah chorus during a service for a widely disliked woman was really asking for sarcastic smiles, after all. Kitty Kirk looked frumpy and gray-faced. Benton and Tippy Chambers stood at attention, but Benton's eyes were cutting all over the sanctuary. He was probably looking for hands to press after the service since politicians never took a day off. Althea Hayes was there, looking sad. Probably thinking about the quick graveside service her husband Tanner was given just days ago. From Myrtle's vantage point she couldn't really see any other faces. Red gave her a hard look and she stopped craning her head around.

Following the service was to be a graveside burial. Judging from the way the sanctuary emptied out ten minutes later, Myrtle doubted there would be anyone in attendance but Cecil and his sister. She noticed they were at the front of the sanctuary, talking to the minister. Parke's daughter looked more and more displeased as Cecil's smirk grew.

"Coming, Myrtle?" asked Elaine, looking at her watch. Red edged toward the sanctuary door.

Myrtle cast another glance at the now-dueling siblings. "I'm going to just sit here for a few minutes." Elaine stared at her, uncomprehendingly. Red gave a gusty sigh and made a shoving, hurry-up motion in the direction of the door to Elaine. Since Elaine was still staring at Myrtle, who had seemed only too eager to leave mere minutes ago, Myrtle repeated, louder, "I'm just going to sit here for a little while."

Red ran a hand through his red hair, standing it up on end. "What are you going on about? We're driving you home and we're leaving now. The service is over, Mama."

"I'll walk home." Now Red was staring at her. "It's a nice day," she said stubbornly. "Besides. I want to pray."

"Pray!?" chorused Elaine and Red.

"Yes," she answered with determination. "I'm an old woman who might not have much time left on this earth. Funerals remind me of the ticking of the clock." She smiled sweetly at Elaine and Red's stunned expressions. "So just leave me." They continued looking at her. "To pray. And then walk." Myrtle pointedly closed her eyes in a pious pose.

Red opened and closed his mouth several times like a guppy while Elaine pulled him towards the sanctuary door. Elaine had her own suspicions about Myrtle's sudden spirituality. She had noticed the feuding siblings at the front of the church, too. It seemed very convenient that Myrtle had picked that moment to speak with God. She knew there was no use changing Myrtle's mind once it was made up, however. She directed her spluttering husband to his car.

Myrtle decided that she would be much more inspired to prayer if she moved closer to the front of the church. She could barely even see the altar where she was from her current vantage point. Cecil and his sister were so deep in debate that they never noticed the gray-haired, big-boned woman moving slowly down the side aisle towards the front. Too bad Methodists didn't kneel. She could really hide, then.

Myrtle leaned close. The words were getting lost in the vaulted ceiling. Or maybe it was Myrtle's ears that were the problem. Whatever the issue, Myrtle wasn't getting good reception. Nathaniel Gluck left minutes ago but probably had an idea what the argument had been about and Myrtle made a mental note to ask him. All she was picking up was angry tones. She moved several more pews up until she was sitting in the same pew that Cecil and his sister had shared. She resumed her prayerful stance. Now the voices came in clearer. Cecil's sister was letting Cecil have it for always taking money from her, not giving anything back, and exposing her to unsavory characters. Myrtle focused more, hoping more would be said about the seedy louts. Her concentration was interrupted by a faraway sneezing that gradually got closer and closer. Opening one eye, she saw Josh Tucker, nose red and eyes watering, making his allergy-ridden way down the aisle. Even his high-volume sneezing didn't disturb the argument, which Myrtle so desperately tried to hear. The preacher, Nathaniel Gluck, re-entered the sanctuary and stood at a short distance looking out of place.

"Sorry Mrs. Clover," wheezed Josh. "Roses just kill me. Can't breathe. Think I left something in the pew. Can't remember exactly where I was sitting, though. Know I sat up front. Hmm."

"No problem," said Myrtle in an icy voice, hoping he'd take the hint and go away. He seemed to be in no hurry to leave however, and apparently had no compunctions about interrupting her prayer life as he scrabbled around, sneezing the whole time. She wondered if Josh were actually doing the same thing she was. She glowered at him. Probably trying to pick up some gossip for a lurid story in the *Bradley Bugle*. Cecil and Cecilia's argument wound down just as Josh finally made his noisy departure. Typical.

She did register one phrase—*nosy old woman* in Cecil's derisive voice, which reached her ears easily. Maybe he planned it that way. *She's just praying!* came his sister's voice angrily. Myrtle kept her head bowed and eyes devoutly closed. She opened an eye when she heard someone plop down next to her on the pew. It was Cecil, still smirking. Cecilia rolled her eyes and started gathering up her things, presumably to get ready to go to the cemetery for the burial. "Mrs. Clover? Hate to disturb your meditation." His smile (not really much of one anyway) didn't reach his eyes.

Myrtle cleared her throat. "Funerals always remind me how close I am to joining the dearly departed. I was moved to prayer to set things right with the Almighty. So sorry about your poor mother, Cecil."

Cecil raised his dark eyebrows. "Why would you be? No one else is. Mother was always making trouble, you know. Everyone hated her." He smiled at the preacher, still hovering uncertainly in the background as he waited to escort them to the cemetery.

"Just the same, it must have been a shock, Cecil. When did you hear the news?" Myrtle asked.

"It was a shock to my system to be awakened before 11:30 on a Saturday, yes. The police make an effective alarm clock."

"So you were asleep when your mother was murdered then?" Myrtle bit her lip. That came out more plainly than she'd planned, but Cecil didn't look surprised. Probably pleased his labeling of her as a nosy old woman was so spot-on.

Nathaniel now seemed very worried as he hovered, looking like a nervous dove in his white pastoral raiment. Instinct told Myrtle she should call him on it. "Something wrong, Nathaniel?"

He hesitated, then said, "I did see your motorcycle at the church that morning, Cecil. Perhaps you ...?" He trailed off, unable to think of a good excuse for the motorcycle's appearance at the church.

Cecilia spoke up, her voice harsh again. "Hitting her up for cash again, were you? Or maybe hitting her up in a totally different way?"

Now Cecil's lips pulled back into a snarl. "Well, that would have been stupid, wouldn't it? Because we both know her money goes to her precious charities and precious Sissy. I'd get a lot more from Mother alive than dead." He picked up his car keys and rose from the pew. "I was there, okay? I asked her for money and she gave me whatever she had in her purse. And she was very much alive when I left her."

Myrtle watched as Cecil quickly left the church, his sister calling angrily out to him as she followed, and Nathaniel trailing miserably behind them.

Chapter Nine

Shortly after being kidnapped by Erma, Myrtle devised an avoid-Erma campaign. The brief break she'd had when Erma left town on the senior bus to gamble had only whetted her appetite for more. Her current tactic of avoiding her neighbor involved looking through her curtains for several minutes for lurking Ermas before leaving, speedy retrieval of all mail delivery, and using caller ID to screen calls.

Myrtle spent some time spying through her sheer curtains. She noticed the Pilgrim (as she'd come to think of him) scurrying to his car and back indoors just as furtively as she did. Could be signs of intelligent life. Maybe he'd picked up on Erma's less-endearing qualities in the past week. Or could he just be tired of the predatory pack of wily widows that descended on him at every opportunity. Myrtle couldn't help noticing that he had ignored his doorbell several times when a courting casserole-bearer had arrived on his porch. And judging from the lights on long after most midnights, he seemed to be up at night as much as Myrtle herself was. Could he be a fellow insomniac? It was nice to know others were burning the midnight oil.

Myrtle sat in her kitchen, drinking coffee and smiling smugly. These precautions had worked amazingly well and consequently Myrtle had enjoyed an Erma-free life for over a week now. It must be killing Erma to keep all her gossip bottled up. Myrtle's eyes glittered gleefully.

But she hadn't counted on Erma using the postal service. One morning Myrtle received a letter. It was actually less a letter than a diatribe. Erma lamented that her ill-health the preceding week—Myrtle fumed at her wasted efforts—had kept her inside and unable to visit Myrtle. "I would hate to pass along my bad cold to you, dear Myrtle. Colds can be so hard on the elderly."

Erma noted that she'd tried to phone Myrtle when she was *sure* Myrtle was home. ("You could be going deaf, Myrtle dear.") Then she launched into a scathing narrative of innuendo and bile ("Warn Red to really investigate Cecil Stockard. That buzzard was circling his mom months ago,") and ending with "Sodom and Gomorrah were pristine in God's eyes compared to Bradley, North Carolina. This town is going to hades in a handbasket! Fondly, Erma."

Myrtle cursed, crumpled the violet-bordered paper and tossed it inaccurately towards her wastebasket, making her curse again. She picked up her cane and thumped toward the front door. She would go to the *Bradley Bugle* office and continue her investigating. Clearly it was impossible to avoid the woman since her insidious evil was capable of reaching her anywhere.

With murder already on her mind, Myrtle glared at her front lawn. Erma's weed collection stretched over the boundaries of her yard and crept into Myrtle's, infesting it with clover, crabgrass, chickweed, and dandelion. She'd complained about it to Erma several weeks ago, and Erma had only shrugged and said, "It's green, Myrtle. And you won't have to worry about watering it." Erma had also bought one of those bug zappers at the hardware store and staked it right on the edge of her property. Naturally this attracted a swarm of everything with wings from all over the neighborhood. That's all Myrtle needed—imported mosquitoes migrating from other yards.

Myrtle entertained black thoughts of sneaking over to Erma's in the middle of the night and planting kudzu in an obscure section of Erma's yard. Considering how fast the weed grew, her house would be engulfed by the time Erma woke up the next morning. She dug at a patch of chickweed with the bottom of her cane, and leaned over to pick up the batch to toss it by the curb. A stray squirrel from Erma's assortment watched her with interest.

A shriek cut through the humid air, causing Myrtle to wobble off-balance and fall forward. She reached out with her hand to catch herself before being yanked roughly up by a pair of large hands. She found herself face to face with a beaming Erma. "Well, aren't I your guardian angel, Myrtle? You'd have broken a hip if I hadn't been here," exclaimed Erma, overlooking the fact that she'd caused Myrtle to stumble in the first place.

Myrtle tried to pull away, but Erma had clamped her big hands around both arms. "I am *so* glad to see you. I was starting to worry you'd fallen down in your house somewhere and couldn't get up again, just like the commercials. Thought I might have to break in! Maybe it would be a good idea for me to have a key to your house, Myrtle. As a precaution."

Myrtle shuddered. "I'll be fine, Erma. Red is right across the street. Can't do any better than having the chief of police just a stone's throw away."

Erma opened her mouth to say something and Myrtle started walking, "Wish I could stay and talk, but I've got some business to take care of in town." Erma was still talking as Myrtle walked off, but Myrtle ignored her and kept going. Erma would chalk up her rudeness to deafness anyway.

THE *Bradley Bugle* newspaper office was where papers went to die. Because it was filled to overflowing with notebooks, reference books, loose-leaf paper, and photographs that had apparently never been purged, it was a sanctuary for pulp. Sloan Jones, the editor, knew where everything was. *Bugle* readers would walk in off the street looking for a picture of the Scout float in the 4th of July parade from ten years ago or some such thing. Sloan would tap a beefy finger against his ever-expanding forehead, think a second while humming a fragment of a tune, walk unerringly to the stack, and pull it out from the pile.

By the looks of things, Josh Tucker had only added to the mass of mess in the newspaper office. But he made the paper more respectable. Not every little town had a former *New York Times* reporter on staff, after all. Josh ran out of Bradley just as fast as he could after graduation, he was that ready to escape. Myrtle felt the same urge every time she ran into one of his parents. They bragged their heads off: Josh-this, Josh-that. It was enough to drive you crazy. Why he ever came back to Bradley if he was such a big-shot in New York, Myrtle couldn't figure.

In the middle of the piles of paper, books, and pictures on Sloan's desk was a makeshift shrine for a large trophy. Myrtle supposed the pointed thing on top of the granite base was supposed to depict a quill pen. It looked more like a syringe to Myrtle. Sloan was slavishly devoted to the trophy and the reporter responsible for receiving it.

"Where's Wonder Boy?" asked Myrtle, stomping over to Sloan. He'd barely acknowledged her entrance into the *Bugle*, just giving a grunted greeting and continuing proofing the copy on his crowded desk.

"Hmm? Oh. Josh is out covering the Parke Stockard story." Sloan rubbed his high forehead with a fleshy hand and shook his head in admiration. "Maybe he'll solve the case. I guess he'd be the guy to do it." Sloan noticed Myrtle's ill-concealed grumpiness and hastily added, "Not that Red can't, Miss Myrtle. No ma'am." Sloan had many bad memories from high school as the focus of Miss Myrtle's wrath. He had no desire to regenerate it now.

If he'd hoped to placate her, he was wrong. Myrtle said, "I was thinking more of *my* solving the case, Sloan." At his blank expression, she added, "It's basically just a cerebral exercise, you know."

Sloan became very busy at his desk, pushing some stacks of paper one way and pulling others another. "Right. Okay."

"So during the curse of my investigation, I mean the *course* of my investigation ..." She squinted suspiciously at Sloan when he made a strange hiccupping sound. "I needed to find out some information on Benton Chambers and his dealings with Parke Stockard."

Sloan looked suddenly serious. "You're not poking around into Benton Chambers' business are you, Miz Clover? He's one of our biggest advertisers. All those election ads." Sloan gazed sadly at the open window as if he could see money floating out of his newsroom and back into Benton Chambers' pocket.

"I'm just trying to get at the *truth*, Sloan." She used her best schoolmarm voice and watched Sloan slump in his seat.

"Well, it's no harm telling you, I guess. Not like it has anything to do with it."

Sloan absently pushed his water glass to one side and trailed his finger through the water ring he unearthed. He hesitated again, looking plaintively at Myrtle. She coughed peremptorily and he sighed and said, "Benton Chambers is running for re-election on the platform of more diligent zoning and possibly even a moratorium on development."

"That part I knew, Sloan. It's on all his campaign flyers."

Sloan stared at his forefinger as if wondering how it had gotten wet. He rubbed it absently on his wrinkled button-down shirt. "Parke wasn't happy and talk is she pressured Benton to embrace the development." Thinking about the lovely, dead Parke prompted a gusty sigh.

"But why would that bother Benton? So she wouldn't vote for him. Big deal—one vote."

Sloan pulled at his shirt collar. "Right." Under Myrtle's penetrating stare, he blurted, "Talk is that Parke Stockard had some info on Benton Chambers. Something he didn't want made public."

Myrtle thought back to her conversation with Shelia in the diner. This seemed to corroborate her story that Parke knew he was having an affair with someone other than herself.

"Who exactly is behind this talk?"

Sloan shifted his eyes away and shrugged. Probably Wonder Boy. She made a mental note to talk to Josh Tucker about what rumors he'd unearthed.

"So Parke Stockard might have threatened to reveal Benton's secret, ruining his bid for re-election and his reputation if he didn't support her development project."

Sloan shrugged again. "I think you're barking up the wrong tree, Miss Myrtle. Maybe you should be taking a closer look at her son, Cecil. Now he's a piece of work, let me tell you." He was still smarting from an ugly comment Cecil made to him a couple of weeks ago.

"Word has it," he said, "that Cecilia is kicking smirking Cecil out of Parke's house."

"Banished from Eden, hmm?"

"More like run out on a rail. His gambling really got her goat, and she thinks he conned her momma out of all kinds of money." Sloan gave a satisfied smile at the idea of Cecil Stockard in a dinky apartment eating cans of baked beans.

"I don't see Parke getting conned out of anything. She just had a soft spot for Cecil."

Sloan glanced up at the wall clock, remembering his deadline. "What about your column, Miss Myrtle? Can't slack off on your day job to play detective."

Myrtle said icily, "I suppose you *do* have some space to fill now that Parke's column is gone. Don't you have enough copy from trophy-winning Wonder Boy?" She scowled at the large trophy of a quill pen that was glorified on Sloan's desk.

Sloan's jowls fell with desperation now and he said, "Well, I was going to have to edit her column anyway. After all, you had a much bigger following than Parke Stockard. People just eat up your articles." Myrtle frowned at him. "Like the nose bleed and leg cramp tips?"

Myrtle said, "I happen to have some great tips this week. Very *useful* hints on sharpening garbage disposal blades."

Sloan knit his brows.

"By putting ice cubes in the disposal and running it," continued Myrtle.

Sloan shuddered. "Tell the readers not to stick their hands in there. All we need is to get sued because some bozo stuck his hand in the blades to see how sharp they were."

Myrtle was giving a dismissive sniff for effect when she caught the faint scent of cigarette smoke and she remembered the scent of smoke in the sanctuary. She leveled Sloan with a serious look that froze him in his seat. "Have you started smoking again?"

Sloan had the grace to look guilty. "Only when I'm drinking, Miss Myrtle."

"Considering there's a half-empty bottle of Jim Beam and a glass on the desk, that's not very comforting." A blush crept across his jowly features and Myrtle asked, "What about Won—um—Josh? Is he a smoker?"

Sloan snorted. "No, he's the cleanest-living newsman I've ever come across. No vices as far as I can tell. And he lived in

New *York*. Gotham City!" Sloan shook his head—whether in admiration or disgust, Myrtle couldn't tell.

"Could you give me Josh's cell phone number?" asked Myrtle.

Sloan looked uncertain.

"Since he's such a fantastic writer, maybe he could give me some tips to improve my column," said Myrtle.

Myrtle hoped Sloan wouldn't see through her lie. After all, it should be *obvious* that her column didn't need any improvement. She had nothing to worry about, though—Sloan was in total agreement about Josh's extraordinary talent. He gave her the number, which Myrtle dialed on her way out the door. After all, Josh could have a useful perspective on the case, as much as she hated to admit it. He is both an old-timer and newcomer to Bradley.

He quickly picked up. "Josh Tucker here."

"Josh. It's Myrtle Clover." She thought she detected a sigh on the other end of the line.

"What can I do for you, Mrs. Clover?"

"I wanted to meet with you for a little while tomorrow and maybe pick your brains about the case."

Now the sigh was clearly audible, even to Myrtle's elderly ears. "You know I'd really love to, Mrs. Clover. But I'm a little busy right now."

Myrtle adopted a wheedling tone. "It would really mean a lot to me. Your mom and dad are such good friends of mine," (the lie made her wince) "and I'd love a chance to catch up with you. Plus, I've found out some information, myself. I can give you a tip." Now all she had to do was come up with something to tell him tomorrow. Well, it could be any kind of dingy-batty thing. She was old, after all.

Josh still seemed uncertain about whether this would be a wise investment of his precious time. "A tip concerning what, exactly?"

"Well, something I was talking with Kitty about. Yes."

Now she thought she heard a groan. Maybe Kitty, crazy as she was these days, wasn't exactly the best person to use in her story. She should have thought of saying that Red had given her some information. "Okay, Mrs. Clover," he said soothingly. "Maybe we can meet up for a late lunch. At Bo's Diner?"

And another helping of heart-attack-on-a-plate. Well, she'd lived this long. "I'll meet you there!" Myrtle was all smiles when she hung up the phone. If there was anyone who knew anything about the case, it would be Mr. Investigative Reporter. It could mean a real break in the case. As she was walking home, she suddenly had an idea. She looked at Josh's cell phone number, which Sloan had written down for her. It had sounded familiar and now she knew where. She pulled out the old receipt from her pocketbook where she'd written down the numbers Parke had called from her cell phone. Parke had called Josh Tucker the morning she was murdered.

At home, Myrtle couldn't stop thinking about the case. She really *did* need a sidekick. All the detectives in books and movies had them. It would be helpful if her sidekick could have a younger back and feet, too. She decided to give Elaine a call and mull over the case with her.

Myrtle was about to hang up the phone after it rang on Elaine's end eight times when a harried "hello" came through.

There was wailing in the background that sounded like Jack, some harsh French that Myrtle assumed was cursing, and what sounded like a wild animal going through death throes. "Wrong number!" said Myrtle, reaching over to put the phone back on the hook.

"Myrtle? Is that you?"

"That's what I should be asking *you*! You don't sound like yourself. Is everything okay? What's that ruckus?"

"Oh god. Jack got into a jar of Mentholatum."

"I'll call Poison Control!"

"Hmm? No, he didn't eat it. He smeared the whole jar over his hair." Elaine seemed to be running away from the chaos, since the loud noises were rapidly receding into the background. "And Jean-Marc. Well, he tried to help with the laundry. All the baby stuff, you know, makes a lot of laundry. I really appreciate his help," she said convincingly. "But the washer got out of balance and tried to walk out the door." She gave a giggle that sounded more like a sob.

"Jean-Marc tried to walk out the door?"

"No, the washer. It's thumping around and walking. But it might unplug itself soon."

"I can call you back later." Myrtle felt desperate now. Stress radiated through the phone and she was right in the line of fire.

"Did you need something?"

"It was nothing." Myrtle knew she was going to be tackling this case alone. Red was right; Elaine had too much going on.

Chapter Ten

Myrtle glared at the bunny crack on her ceiling again. Telling yourself to go to sleep wasn't any good when you weren't used to following orders. Time for her warm milk nightcap. She tossed the covers off and headed for the kitchen.

She poured the milk from the pan into her glass and stepped out on her screen porch. It was surprisingly cool tonight, not like the humid, buggy nights they usually had this time of year. She looked down the wooded hill leading to the lake and the rickety dock. She used to go down to the lake on nights she couldn't sleep and sit on the dock to watch the water and listen to the night animals calling each other and the water lapping up against the sides of the dock. She even had a rocking chair out there just for that purpose, although she hadn't gone down there for a while.

She looked longingly out at the dark water, then picked up her cane and a flashlight. The full moon would light her way down the hill, too. A little milk, a little rocking by the lake and she'd be ready to sleep the rest of the night.

She thought she heard a rustling in the bushes when she stepped out into the yard. Probably one of Erma's pet squirrels she thought. Or a snake. But she'd rather think about the squirrels instead.

The path leading down to Myrtle's dock had, in more active days, been worn into a dirt trail with knobby tree roots intermittently allowing themselves to be stairs. Now, with more infrequent use, the path was getting overgrown. Myrtle brought a flashlight, but the moon provided enough light for her to leave it off. The dock had seen better days, too; it was faded to a gray wood with lots of knotholes. Red wasn't thrilled about her forays down to the dock—since it was a floating dock, it bobbed around a bit. Every once in a while, though, Myrtle liked to sit there and look at the water and feel the breeze off the lake. The weathered rocking chair on the dock was there for that very reason, although Myrtle was sure that if Red realized she was rocking on the dock in the middle of the night, it would be quickly dispatched back up to her screened porch.

Myrtle settled into the old chair and rocked slowly, mulling over the case. What was Althea hiding? She was evasive and vague whenever Myrtle saw her. And Cecil, the stereotypical bad guy. How easy it would be to peg him as the killer, considering all his other undesirable traits. Is that something the real murderer would count on, though, and use to their advantage?

Myrtle heard a noise behind her and the hair on the back of her neck stood up. She was about to whirl around when she felt a vicious shove aimed at the middle of the rocking chair back. As the chair thumped onto the dock, Myrtle felt herself fly though the air and into the water. After a second of blind panic, she worked her way out of her heavy bathrobe and kicked through the murky water to clutch a white bumper hanging from the dock. She caught her breath, then pushed her way through to the shore. The water wasn't deep, thanks to the persistent drought for several summers. Dripping wet, she shivered despite the warm night and looked fearfully around for her attacker.

The curved path leading up to her house looked more ominous now with the many pine trees and azalea bushes on its sides offering many places to hide. She plodded up onto the dock, soaking wet and shivering with shock. Picking up her cane from the floor of the dock, she turned to go back up the hill to her house. She heard rustling in the bushes ahead and her heart slammed into her ribcage as a dark shape loomed out of the darkness. She held her cane out like a shotgun and called, "Who's there! *Who is there?*"

An older man of about 70 years with steel-gray hair, wire-rimmed glasses, and a concerned expression approached her cautiously.

"The pilgrim!" gasped Myrtle with relief. He looked at her with concern.

"Gone for a swim? Miss Myrtle, isn't it?" Wasn't a very good idea, was it? Why don't we just go inside and find a warm drink, dry clothes, and a telephone? Who is in charge of ... uh ... who should I call?"

"Call the police. And my son. They're the same."

An inquisitive yoo-hoo reached their ears. "Myrtle? That you?"

Behind the wire-rimmed glasses, Myrtle saw the panic in the pilgrim's eyes. His reaction to Erma was certainly a sign of intelligence. He pulled her silently along the path and quickly into

Myrtle's house. The door closed behind them and Erma Sherman's curtains stirred in the window. She was obviously back from her gambling expedition. Myrtle shivered and her companion pulled a throw off the sofa and put it around her. "Best get changed," he said gruffly. "I'm Miles Bradford, by the way."

"Ah, that explains it," said Myrtle. Miles raised an eyebrow and she answered, "Miles Standish. William Bradford." To her horror, she gave a tremendous hiccup. Good lord, he must think she'd been drinking. She'd swallowed half the lake while she was in there. Shivering, she hurried to her bedroom and heard Miles making the phone call.

A few minutes later (not surprisingly, since Red lived diagonally across the street), Red was in her den, seeming to take up most of it with his restless large frame. His graying red hair stood up on end as if he'd dug his fingers into it. He had on a pair of sweatpants, a pajama top, and a pair of tennis shoes. Erma Sherman must be having a field day. Red introduced himself to Miles, thanked him for helping out his mother, then asked him, "What exactly happened?" He held up his hand to stop Myrtle as she tried to interrupt. "One minute, Mama. I want to hear it from Mr. Bradford first."

"Miles, please. Well, I'm something of an insomniac," (Myrtle smiled smugly as her suspicions were confirmed), "and I was up in my kitchen getting a snack when I saw your mother going down into the woods toward the lake."

Red gritted his teeth, then said, "Go on, please."

"I didn't think too much of it. I thought she might be an insomniac, too, because I'd seen her lights on other nights when I was up and unable to sleep. But a little while later I felt a little bit uneasy. So I hurried down there and saw your mother, sopping wet, coming back up the path and looking at me like she'd seen a ghost."

"Mama, I know this isn't a nice thing to say to a lady, but you're not a spring chicken anymore. Going through the woods on a poorly cleared path to a rickety floating dock after midnight? Pitching into the water, fully dressed?" Red broke off, clearly seeing a Greener Pastures Retirement Home prospect instead of his mother.

"She had her cane with her," vouched Miles. "And waved it threateningly at me. Very convincing," he added to Myrtle, who bowed in response.

Red was pressing on his forehead now as if to offer some counter-pressure to the throbbing he felt inside.

"Besides," said Myrtle, "I didn't pitch into the lake, Red. I was pushed. Hard."

"Tell me everything."

She did, although she didn't know much. All she knew was that she was mulling over life in the rocking chair and the next was flying into the lake. Red and Miles both listened quietly. Miles' expression was shock and puzzlement and Red's was a mix of anger and concern.

"What kind of homicidal hamlet is this? What makes someone fling an elderly woman, sorry, Myrtle, in the lake?" asked Miles.

"She's not just any elderly woman," said Red in a growling tone. "She's Miss Meddlesome Myrtle who messes with murder. And somebody didn't like it."

"There'll be payback," said Myrtle, her words laced with venom.

Red was unimpressed. "Whatcha going to do, Mama? Knock them upside the head with your fat pocketbook? Challenge them to a thumb wrestling match? Cook them supper?" He snickered. The last was really unforgivable. Why Red was under the delusion that Myrtle couldn't cook was beyond her. He could just get used to the gnomes in the front yard because they weren't going anywhere anytime soon. Maybe she even needed to add a couple to her collection.

After a few more questions, Red rubbed his eyes wearily and made motions to leave. He gave his mother an especially tight hug and Myrtle blinked tears away. She knew the night could have gone much differently if she hadn't been so determined to get out of the lake. Miles Bradford told Red he'd stay a while with Myrtle since he wasn't going to be able to go back to sleep anyway. That elicited a spark of curiosity and interest in Red's eyes before he tramped out into the night.

Miles and Myrtle stared at each other. Myrtle was sure she presented quite a sight in her slippers, pajamas and fluffy robe. Her hair was not in its customary carefully-arranged poof, but lay wetly flattened on her head. She didn't feel at all self-conscious, though. And she certainly didn't feel the flutter of heartstrings that the lovelorn ladies camped on his doorstep did. She felt very comfortable, though. Her new neighbor seemed intelligent, capable, and—was still driving. Could this be the Watson she'd been looking for?

She remembered her manners and offered to make her visitor some decaf coffee or tea. He stood up instead. "I'll get it. You probably just need to put your feet up for a little while."

Myrtle settled back on the big pillows on her living room sofa and sighed. Miles said, "Can you fill me in on what's been going on here?"

"Call me Ishmael," said Myrtle. A lesser man would have dug out his cell phone and called Red back to the house. But, being a fan of *Moby Dick*, Miles realized that Myrtle meant that there was quite a story to follow.

So Myrtle told it. She told him all about her investigative prowess and the murder. She told about discovering the body, figuring out likely suspects, and questioning them. She even touched on her lack of a sounding board, Elaine's sudden hectic schedule, and the French exchange student. And Miles Bradford's steady gaze behind his wire-rimmed glasses and serious demeanor made her decide to share even more with him—her suspicions about the suspects, and clues she'd found. Through it all, Miles listened quietly, nodding his head occasionally, or asking a question about something he didn't understand. He got up a couple of times to refill their mugs with coffee.

After she finished talking, they were quiet for a couple of minutes, just thinking and swirling their coffee around. "It sounds like you have some good ideas, Myrtle. I see you get a lot of your information from hearsay, but it seems to work for you." He added slowly, "I'm not sure, though, why you're getting involved. You didn't care a fig about Parke Stockard. And Red and the state police sound perfectly capable."

Myrtle resumed the silence for a moment before answering. "Pure willfulness, I guess. I want to show Red that my brain is still working at full capacity. This case represents a challenge for me. Lately I felt like I was being swept under the rug—like I was supposed to just watch my soaps and have milk and cookies and live on in blissful stagnation."

Miles wondered what his role in all this was supposed to be. Was he just a sounding board or was she looking for some sort of crime-fighting associate? Maybe it was too early for her to know. It looked like she wanted to get some glory from all this and might not want to share the spotlight with him. He decided to just be available, but not pushy. Listen, but not offer too many ideas. And, obviously, not scold her for taking risks. Why *not* take risks at her age?

"Who do you think pushed you into the lake? They obviously spent some time watching your house and saw you leave it. Was there anyone who you've been pushing for information lately that might have wanted to kill you?" he asked.

Myrtle leaned her head on the back of her overstuffed sofa. "I don't really know that they were trying to kill me. They might have just been trying to warn me off. Scare me. Make me long for the soaps, milk, and cookies." She sighed. "I can't believe someone slipped by Erma's eagle eye."

"So you've been nosing around in general. Is there one person over another that you think might have been feeling you were digging too hard?" Miles asked.

"Not really. I spent some time with Kitty Kirk and she's supposedly malicious enough to have given Parke food poisoning. Cecil isn't exactly Mr. Nice Guy, either. But the murderer could easily have picked up on the fact I'm asking a lot of questions and gossiping around town. I guess it could have been anybody. If they're desperate enough to kill, they're desperate enough to push an old lady in a lake." She paused. "We've also got a local politician who's covering up an affair. And running for re-election."

Miles asked, "Who is it?"

Myrtle was positive she caught a glint of interest in his steely eyes. He was looking much more promising as sidekick material.

He leaned toward her, light shining on his glasses. "So?" he asked impatiently.

"So Benton Chambers has a honey that he's meeting up with—right in the middle of nowhere in Crazy Dan Land." Myrtle smirked. It felt great to be the imparter of information.

"Crazy Dan Land? That hubcap place way out in the country?

Myrtle nodded. "Way out in the country is the perfect place for messing around."

"Do you think Parke somehow found out?"

"Bet she did. She seemed like the kind of person who could find out just about anything. It sounds like maybe *she* had a fling with Benton, too. She wouldn't have wanted to use that as her leverage, though—could have damaged her own reputation. But if she had an affair with him, it probably made her realize that he might be cheating with other women, too. It would have been easy enough to tail his car and find out."

Miles still looked dubious. "You think he would actually kill her over that kind of thing?"

Myrtle shot him a condescending look. "You obviously don't understand politics. That's the kind of scandal that could blow an election. Think of all the politicians who have been brought down by matrimonial discord."

Miles asked, "What's he like? Benton's one I haven't met yet." Myrtle looked thoughtful. "Well, for one he's not the person on the Town Council I'd go to with a problem. He's all bluster and swagger and no substance. Plus, he probably drinks too much. He's got that bloated, flushed look."

"So," mused Miles, "Benton follows Parke to the church?" He raised a doubtful eyebrow.

"He would have known she was going to be there. After all, his wife was going to the same church meeting."

Miles inclined his head, granting her the point. "So he meets up with her at the church. Maybe he tries to convince her to keep quiet about his affair."

Myrtle snorted. "He'd have had to use all his persuasive techniques. She was going to use that information as leverage to force him to support her development plan, I bet. Then he'd have to change his platform."

"He pops her on the head and takes off back home. His wife is his alibi?"

Myrtle nodded. "Yes, Tippy said he was home with her. And he said the same. Covering for each other." She sighed.

Miles noticed Myrtle suddenly looked tired and he glanced over at the loudly ticking kitchen wall clock. 3:30. "I'd better get back home. If I stay any longer we'll be the talk of Bradley."

Myrtle made a sour face. "We probably already are. Erma was looking out her curtains when you came in. She'll likely ignore the fact I looked half-drowned and come up with some wild story about Red coming over to defend my honor and you defeating him and staying until the wee hours." She slapped the arm of the sofa with her hand in irritation.

Miles smiled, revealing very nice teeth. "Well, it will probably enhance your reputation if you're so concerned about not looking like a put-to-pasture biddy."

Myrtle brightened. "That's so. Might make things a little more interesting around here." She showed Miles out, then stumbled to bed for a dreamless sleep.

Chapter Eleven

His mother had really done it this time. She had taken leave of her senses, getting involved in his murder investigation. You'd think she had nothing else to do with her time. That she couldn't find any *legitimate* hobbies in the town of Bradley. Perkins was going start thinking that Myrtle Clover was Parke's killer—with boredom as her motive.

Red couldn't figure out why she was so stubborn over this. She was just bound and determined that she was going to crack the case and get some sort of glory or an award or something. Now she'd managed to put herself in mortal danger. And Red was going to have to spend a perfectly good lunch break cutting back her shrubbery to make it villain-proof. He heaved a sigh.

Detective Lieutenant Perkins walked out of Red's office and joined Red in the station lobby. "How's she doing?" he asked in a quiet voice.

Red rolled his eyes. "She's doing just fine and wild to get her bloodhound nose back on the trail. Probably ready to go back out to the lake and look for clues about her attacker. Maybe she'll go back in the middle of the night to recreate the scene."

Red sighed. He took a big gulp from his coffee mug and thought back to his "to do" list. "And I'll take the opportunity to cut back her bushes while she's out of the house. Apparently they're big enough to house all kinds of predators. She's real particular about those shrubs—you'd think they were her children. She never wants more than just a little bit taken off the top, then I end up going back out there to cut more off after a good rain. They need a good pruning this time." He made a hacking motion with his hands that boded ill for Myrtle's shrubbery. "She's going over to see Elaine and the baby this afternoon, so that'll be my chance."

"Doesn't she have a yard man to help her with her yard?"

Red gave a short laugh. "I don't think Dusty does enough work to classify him as a bona fide yard man. The grass is either too wet, too dry, too full of pollen to cut or else the weather is too windy or too hot. And he doesn't do bushes anymore, so I'm the lucky guy with that job. I do everything that Dusty isn't up to doing. Mama hates those yard warriors, so she chose Dusty."

"Yard warriors?"

"Oh, you know them. They're the ones who wake you up on Saturday morning with blowers strapped to their backs and a weed whacker in their hand. Mama says the noise makes her teeth jangle. Dusty's mower is from the 1970s and goes 'putt-putt.' He can't afford the loud yard equipment and he's too puny to pull the start cords, anyway."

"Sounds like a real gem."

"You should meet his wife, Puddin. She does—or doesn't do—Mama's housekeeping."

Perkins watched Red fume for a minute and had the feeling Myrtle's bushes were going to pay the price. He said, "You know, Red, maybe this will be the end of the line for her with the case. It must have scared her to death to have been thrown into the lake like that. She could have broken a bone with the impact, or even drowned. Surely that's got to give her second thoughts about continuing on with the case."

"It would give a *normal* octogenarian woman second thoughts. No, strike that. A *normal* octogenarian woman wouldn't be involved with a murder case." Red sighed. "Maybe you're right. This could be it. I'm hoping there's a romantic interest in her life now. Her rescuer was a new neighbor who lives a couple of doors down from her."

"Sounds promising."

"We'll see," said Red glumly. "Even if they're just friends, maybe it'll be enough to distract her from snooping."

Myrtle *was* distracted from snooping, but only because her turn at Altar Guild was up again. This trip to the church had not proven nearly as eventful and was spent actually arranging flowers with Kitty Kirk, who was back to creating simple arrangements, during a conversation about updating the sound system in the church. She really was going to have to tell Nathaniel that the Altar Guild wasn't really her thing. Otherwise she'd be sticking flowers in vases until she was dead and buried.

Her mind wandered while Kitty and the other ladies talked. Being in the sanctuary reminded her of the funeral. She wondered again about Cecil Stockard. He had such a sly, sneaky air about him. But could he have been angry enough with his mother to kill her in cold blood? She could see him wheedling her. She could even picture him stealing money from her. But Cecil Stockard—guilty of matricide? She couldn't believe he had the guts to kill his mother. He seemed much more of a backhanded type than a bludgeon-you-with-an-offering-plate-from-close-up type. A stray glance toward her yard stopped her dead in her tracks.

"What on *earth* did Red do to my bushes?" she shrieked to herself. She hurried into her house and punched the numbers with a shaking finger. "What did Red do to my bushes?" she demanded into the phone.

Elaine, who was trying to scrape very thick, dark coffee crud from the bottom of the coffee carafe and trying to forget that Jean-Marc had called American coffee "a punishment", answered, "Hmm?"

"Red! My bushes!"

"Oh," said Elaine. Myrtle wasn't supposed to know that Red was trying to get fired by Myrtle as her makeshift yardman. "Did he do a bad job with them?"

"A massacre would have been an improvement," said Myrtle.

"The bushes are that bad?" Elaine gave a faint smile at Jean-Marc as he sauntered into the kitchen. He raised his eyebrows with interest at her stressed tone and walked over to the window, pulling the mini-blinds out of the way. Elaine heard a French oath, followed by what sounded like his usual opinion: "abominable!" Jean-Marc whirled around and walked toward Elaine. "Permit me?" he asked, motioning to the phone.

Elaine relinquished the receiver with relief.

"Madame." Elaine could have sworn she saw him give a small bow. "Please allow me to assist in the liberation of your *jardin.*" Apparently Myrtle felt the need to offer a perfunctory protest because he shook his head emphatically. "*Non*. My pleasure." Myrtle spoke for a minute and Jean-Marc grunted an agreement. "*Oui.* I will come then. Your bush-shez will be much improved." He hung up the phone and walked to the window again. "*Zut alors.*"

Elaine stifled her giggle and scrubbed fervently at the coffee pot. Looks like Red had gotten himself off the hook as Myrtle's resident gardener. She only hoped the yard gnomes wouldn't live in the front yard forever. She'd thought that Myrtle had gotten over her grudge, but the gnomes remained. At this rate, they were going to have to start weed-eating around them, and that really *was* going to be a chore.

Myrtle spotted the wall clock and suddenly remembered her lunch date with Josh Tucker. She grabbed her pocketbook and cane and slipped out the door. He'd probably already be there when she arrived, but wouldn't have waited long enough to leave.

She waited a moment for her eyes to adjust from the bright sunshine to the dim interior of the diner. The brown-paneled walls contributed to the dark effect, but Myrtle soon spotted Josh Tucker sitting at a green, Formica-topped table in a vinyl booth. She crossed the shining linoleum floor and Josh stood respectfully until she cautiously sank down onto the low booth.

A waitress in a pink, ruffled apron stopped by the table with a glass of water and handed Josh a plate of fried vegetables. She asked if Myrtle wanted to go ahead and order. Myrtle glanced over the laminated menu, although she knew it by heart. "Just a grilled cheese and fries this time, please." The waitress walked off and Myrtle said, "Sorry I kept you waiting, Josh."

"That's no problem, Miss Myrtle," he said. "I was just starting to get a little worried about you, that's all." He gave her a searching, reporter-like look.

Myrtle hesitated, then decided not to tell him about the attack on her the night before. It didn't actually have anything to do with the reason she was late, and she didn't want it to be publicized and have all the suspects getting their guard up when she was around. It wouldn't help if they all realized she was investigating the case instead of merely being gossipy.

Instead she took a deep breath, inhaling the scent of deep-frying grease. "I just love this place," she said. "Everything tastes a little better when it's fried."

Josh gave a perfunctory smile, which disappeared in the deep lines in his face. "Bo's Diner was one of the places I missed when I was up North. Not that they don't have a ton of places to eat in New York, but no one seemed to cook fried food like Bo. I'd have thought too much was bad for you, but judging from your longevity, maybe I'm wrong." He was quickly delving into the food on his plate, making short work of the food.

Myrtle dismissively waved a hand. "My arteries are clear as a bell." She had been curious about what would make Josh decide to leave the *New York Times* and return to Bradley. "What made you decide to come back home? Did you just miss your hometown, or have your parents been ailing? I haven't seen Martin and Jill for a while."

Josh lifted a beefy hand and smoothed it over his comb-over several times, his hooded, gray eyes revealing nothing. "Mom and Dad are all right. They're just getting older and since I'm their only child, I felt like I should be around in case they needed me. New York isn't all that close to North Carolina, you know."

But it's only a short plane ride, thought Myrtle. Especially when his parents were completely healthy. There must be more to the story than that. "Well, I know that Sloan Jones is happy to have you at the *Bradley Bugle*. He thinks you're a real feather in his cap. Award-winning writer and all that." With difficulty, Myrtle was able to keep the sarcasm out of her voice. She reminded herself not to call him "Wonder Boy." Not to his face, anyway.

Josh gave her a polite smile and then said in a firm tone, "You said you had some information for me?" At Myrtle's blank expression, he prompted, "You said something that you and Kitty had been talking about." He reached into a briefcase and pulled out a miniature tape recorder.

Had she? She remembered with panic that was indeed how she managed to set up this meeting. But the actual purpose was for *her* to get information from *him*. She thought fast. She could always play up the foggy-old-lady angle. Fogginess was pretty believable at her age.

"Yes, Josh, I did discover something from talking to Kitty. I found out," she leaned forward and spoke breathlessly, "that Kitty Kirk had been at the church that morning!" Myrtle sat back and looked at Josh triumphantly and tried not to laugh at his crestfallen face.

He said gently, "But didn't we already know that, Miss Myrtle? She was there early that morning for Altar Guild and was putting the wildflower arrangement out. It doesn't mean she was still there when Parke Stockard was killed. She was supposed to have left and gone back home before coming back to the church for the Women of the Church meeting you arrived for." He stabbed at the last few bites of his veggie plate.

"Oh, did we already know that?" Myrtle adopted a confused look. "But don't you think it's odd that she did the altar guild stuff so early? I mean, I was supposed to help her with the arrangement before the Women of the Church meeting, which was why I was in the sanctuary at all."

He flushed as he always did when he spoke Parke's name. Young love. "She probably wanted to get the flowers set up in the sanctuary before Parke Stockard arrived. Parke was bent on putting in formal arrangements of flowers, you know, and didn't like Kitty's wildflowers."

"The wildflowers which made it easier for you to attend church with your allergies, right? That was kind of Kitty," said Myrtle.

"She's a kind person," said Josh. He looked pointedly at his watch and said, "Was there anything else, Miss Myrtle?"

Now she was going to have to stall for time. "Actually, there is something, Josh. I was hoping you could do something about the way the *Bugle* does the obituary page."

Josh looked longingly at the door and pushed his comb-over off his large forehead.

"I mentioned it to Sloan before, of course, and he did absolutely nothing about it. It just drives me nuts, looking at the obituaries every week and seeing those smiling faces beaming out at me. Like the deceased are grinning right at me and saying,

'We're just so *delighted* to be dead, thanks for asking.' Don't you think we could have a no-picture policy? Give the dead folks some dignity?"

Josh gave a sour-looking smile. "I'll see what I can do, Miss Myrtle. Now I really do have to be going."

The waitress came back with Myrtle's grilled cheese. Myrtle quickly figured out what she wanted to ask Josh while he was caught off guard. "I was wondering, Josh," said Myrtle, "if you'd been at the church that morning, too." She took a deep breath and lied, "Someone mentioned they'd seen you driving up or back or something." She smiled apologetically for her fuzziness.

A look flashed in his hooded eyes that she couldn't really read—was it irritation?—then he replied, "That's what happens when you live in a small town: everybody knows your business. I *was* over there that morning, as Sloan is especially aware of since he set it up. He assigned me to take some pictures and get a few quotes from the Women of the Church meeting for the "Around Town" piece. I got to the church early, went over to the dining hall, started setting up, then realized I didn't have my flash with me. So I left to go back home. When I came back, there was a mob at the church, Red's police car was parked by the sanctuary, and I ended up with a much better article than the Women of the Church piece. End of story, Miss Myrtle." His voice was gentle, but his unhappy mouth tugged downward as usual. He reached over and turned off his tape recorder, signifying the end of the interview.

The tape recorder and the professionalism it indicated irritated Myrtle. She pulled out her own tape recorder from her pocketbook and showed it to Josh. "You're not the only one who carries one around. I find it's *so* helpful when I'm talking to people for my tip column. Sometimes they'll just stop me in the street with a tip . . . you know how popular my column is. If I didn't carry this around with me I'd forget half the tips people have given me."

But Josh seemed to have stopped listening. Myrtle opened her mouth to ask another question when she noticed an arrested look on Josh's face. She turned and also froze when she saw Erma Sherman coming through the door. "Yoo hoo!" Erma called to them, causing people from other tables to turn around. "Miss Myrtle and Josh! Myrtle, are you gonna hog *all* the eligible bachelors in town?"

Josh gave an agonized groan and said, "Got to run, Miss Myrtle. My lunch hour is over." He nodded to Erma on his way out the door, careful to wend his way around the tables as far away from Erma Sherman as possible.

Myrtle crammed the last couple of bites of grilled cheese sandwich and fries down her throat and grabbed her grease-stained check. When she slid her cane towards her, she knocked her pocketbook over, spilling the contents all over the vinyl booth and linoleum floor. Erma had swooped down on her by that time, shoving her out of the way (nearly pushing Myrtle over in the process), and was grabbing handfuls of Myrtle's things and stuffing them back in the purse. Her mouth ran the entire time.

"Happens to everyone, doesn't it? Just when you think you've got your purse, things start jumping out of it. So you've been having lunch with Josh? How nice." Myrtle noticed Erma seemed even more agitated than usual. She *couldn't* think that

Myrtle had designs on Josh? He was almost forty years her junior! But then, if Erma was delusional enough to think that Josh might fancy her, anything was possible.

"I'm sorry I have to run, Erma, but I have stuff to do. Thanks for helping me with my pocketbook." And off she scurried like a rabbit from a hunter, paying for her lunch at the front counter while Erma found some other people to victimize.

The walk from downtown to her house was a short one, but it took a while with the combination of the heat and a full stomach working against her. Besides, she wasn't looking forward to seeing her poor, scalped shrubbery again. Why Red had decided to wreak havoc on the poor things she didn't know.

When she reached her house, though, she was in for a nice surprise. Actually, she was in for a miraculous makeover. Jean-Marc had carefully shaped the bushes, delicately thinning some out, smoothing out the rough edges and mangled bits that Red had left, until the entire effect was well-manicured.

Myrtle smiled at the restoration of normalcy in her yard. Actually, the bushes were much *better* than normal. Jean-Marc had a pleased smile on his face which replaced his usual smirk. Myrtle wondered if the smirk was just a way of dealing with feeling uncomfortable. Feeling uncomfortable must be a constant state of affairs when you're in a different country, experiencing different foods, entertainment, and culture. And when you're busily breaking every household appliance, of course.

"Jean-Marc, I have to admit, I'm amazed. The bushes are *tres belles*. You've done a wonderful job. I really didn't think you could do anything with it."

He nodded but looked as if he hadn't been surprised by his success at all. "Eet was nothing. But the trimmer? The saw? Eet is broken." He shrugged. "Eet was a casualty in the battle of the good versus the evil."

Myrtle gave a hooting laugh. "I should give you a tip for that alone. It'll teach Red not to take out his frustrations on my shrubbery anymore." She rooted in her pocketbook for her purse, but Jean-Marc waved her away.

"Eet was a pleasure," he said as he walked across the street to Red and Elaine's house.

Myrtle smiled after him, then jumped at a voice from behind her. She relaxed when she saw it was Miles Bradford and not Erma still stalking her.

"Sorry I made you jump," he said. "I just wanted to make sure you didn't have any ill effects from last night."

"No, not a thing. Except the fact my bushes were annihilated by a mad pruner this morning."

Miles looked confused and Myrtle said, "Oh, Red cut them way back. I guess he thought killers were lurking in them and ready to jump out at me at any moment. Or else he was just trying to get back at me for getting him out of bed last night. But the exchange student staying with Red and Elaine is apparently some sort of French gardening whiz kid, so they look a lot better."

"Have you done anymore investigating today?" asked Miles.

"I haven't had any luck. I tried to find out some information from Wonder Boy today, but he was playing his cards too close to his chest. Probably going for another award-winning expose." She frowned darkly.

"Wonder Boy?"

"Oh. Josh from the *Bugle*. I thought I might be able to get him to talk about what he's found out, but he went all close-mouthed on me. I did find out that he had been at the church that morning."

"Before the murder?" asked Miles.

"That's what he says. He was in the church hall that morning to take some pictures for the *Bugle* of the Women of the Church meeting. You know, a typical society-type thing. Well, society for the town of Bradley anyway. But he forgot his flash, so he had to go back home. When he came back, Red's police car was parked outside and the hordes had arrived. So he started taking pictures. And sneezing. Which seems to be his usual reaction to churches," said Myrtle.

Myrtle was losing Miles again. "He's allergic to churches?"

"No, he's allergic to roses. Which is one reason why Kitty Kirk's Altar Guild arrangements always had wildflowers. Parke changed all that, of course. Had to have formal arrangements and allergies certainly didn't matter."

"So Josh hated Parke, too?"

"I wouldn't say that. I kind of think he had a crush on her, actually. He always gets this kind of sweet blush whenever someone brings up her name. She was a beautiful woman, even if she was mean as a snake."

"But they never had a relationship?" asked Miles.

"I doubt it. He wasn't in her league when it came to looks. He's got those round shoulders and a stoop. And he always seems to be sweating out of his comb-over."

"Sounds like a real winner," said Miles.

Myrtle looked at her watch. "Well, I've got to get back home. Otherwise tongues will wag. I've been here twenty minutes already and another ten would be scandalous."

Miles walked with her through her yard to her front door and Myrtle said, "Do me a favor? Next time my bushes are getting butchered, please give me a call. Inquiring minds want to know."

Chapter Twelve

The next morning Myrtle scraped her burnt toast over the sink. She slathered it with butter and sat in her sunny kitchen, tapping her pen against the newspaper as she struggled with the crossword. Ordinarily she could knock out the puzzle in minutes and was confident enough to wage her daily attack with an ink pen. Today's puzzle, however, had a wicked number of Russian geography clues. The red pen she used made the paper look as if it had been in battle, judging from the number of blots and scratched out attempts on the page. Myrtle finally pushed the paper away and stood to get another cup of coffee. She couldn't get the Parke Stockard murder out of her mind and there apparently wasn't room enough in her brain for both the murder and the crossword.

What she really wanted to do was to corner Althea and try to get some information from her. She'd never known her to be so exclusive and evasive. She had to know something. She couldn't forget the look on Althea's face when Red had asked what she was doing in the sanctuary. She'd had just such an odd expression, sort of a combination of guilt and fear. Either she had an idea who had done it and was covering up (especially since she'd had her own bone to pick with Parke), or else she'd murdered Parke herself. Myrtle couldn't really picture Althea whacking Parke over the head with a communion plate, but stranger things had happened and Althea certainly had been both distraught and angry about Tanner's death. She also wanted to hear more about Althea's conversations with her nephew Josh regarding his problems with Parke.

What did she really know about Althea, after all? Yes, she'd *known* her for the past 65 years, since Althea was a child. But Althea wasn't a contemporary of Myrtle's and wasn't exactly the most forthcoming person in the world. Althea's idea of a good time was probably to sit inside her old home on the Boulevard and dust the portraits of her dead ancestors. And she was as stubborn as her husband Tanner had been. She wouldn't have taken kindly to a suggestion that she leave her home. Tanner had grown up in the house after all. And she doubted that Parke had approached them with any tact. Parke had thought a lot of herself and apparently figured her considerable beauty was persuasion enough.

Myrtle hesitated for a minute, her hand hovering over the telephone before finally picking up the receiver and dialing Elaine. Althea might be trying to avoid Myrtle's snoopiness, but she would have no reason to avoid a visit with Elaine. Maybe Elaine could trump up some sort of book club excuse to drop by.

Fortunately, life seemed relatively calm at Elaine's. "Hi Myrtle! What's up?" She listened to Myrtle for a couple of minutes, then said cautiously, "Well, you know Red wouldn't like to hear about you doing this, Myrtle. Especially after your being thrown in the lake and everything."

"I was hoping," said Myrtle delicately, "that he wouldn't have to hear anything about it. Isn't there something you need to drop by Althea's? Maybe even a casserole, since she's so recently lost Tanner?"

"Well, but it's past the normal casserole-giving window. Besides, I've taken over a couple of chicken divans."

"Or something for book club?" pleaded Myrtle.

"No-ooo. That's not exactly a paperwork-heavy club, you know. And she hasn't missed any meetings."

Elaine was quiet for a second, then said reluctantly, "She has been asking me to bring Jean-Marc by. She apparently lived in Paris for a while when she was young. I think she wanted to talk to him about France."

"Bingo!" Myrtle dropped the phone in her excitement. "See how easy that is? Can you call and set up a time to drop by this afternoon? And I can just tag along with you."

Elaine wondered if Jean-Marc was inducement enough for Althea to suffer through a visit with Myrtle. She might just shut the door in all their faces. Althea sure had been keen on avoiding Myrtle at all costs lately. It could make for an interesting visit.

IT ENDED UP BEING A close call. Althea opened her door wide and greeted them with delight when Elaine rang the doorbell. But she drew back into her shell when she spotted Myrtle standing behind them. "I—uh—have Myrtle today, Miss Althea," said Elaine, feeling as though she babysitting an extra kid. "I hope that will be okay."

At that moment, perhaps picking up on Althea's anxiety, a monstrous dog lunged out the door and gnashed its considerable teeth at her while strings of drool fell out of its mouth as if it could only imagine the tasty treat that Myrtle would provide. Althea called to it sternly, "Bambi! Down!"

Bambi. Sure.

Althea's interest in Jean-Marc won out over her desire to keep away from Myrtle and she reluctantly invited the group inside. Elaine carried Jack in, looking anxiously over at Bambi as she walked. Althea opened the glass doors at the back of her library and Bambi obediently trotted through them. The antique-filled library was surprisingly untidy for such a neat and tidy person. Althea mumbled an apology, looking around as though she were seeing the disarray for the first time. She pushed some papers out of the way on the leather sofa and sat down, patting a spot next to her for Jean-Marc to sit.

Althea looked wistfully at Jean-Marc. "I have always loved France," she said in a sad voice. She smiled at Jean-Marc. "I took *Le Monde* for the longest time. They had to mail it to me, of course, and the news was ages old. But I felt a real connection to France that way. Reading the paper. My French is too rusty now. My absence from France has been too long."

Jean-Marc nodded sympathetically. "It is the best place. Anywhere."

Elaine got that eager expression on her face that Myrtle grew to understand meant that she was going to make a statement of some kind in French. "France is the most!" she said in French.

Jean-Marc looked at Elaine with an expression that translated into disdain in any language. He muttered something in French that Myrtle thought sounded vaguely like a threat involving their digital camera. Elaine urged him to respond. "You are my tree!" she exclaimed in French and smiled warmly at Jean-Marc. He scowled and muttered darkly.

Althea urged. "Tell me about a wonderful restaurant in Paris." He shrugged eloquently and grunted something that sounded suspiciously like 'McDonalds.' Myrtle hoped they weren't going to lose his interest too early in the visit.

Althea was charmed by the foreign invasion. She persisted in asking questions—with Elaine as occasional interpreter when Althea drew a blank. Myrtle shifted in the Queen Anne chair, tapping her fingers on one of its arms. She had to get off the subject of France...not only for investigative purposes, but also to calm Jean-Marc, who was probably plotting angrily against any number of household electronics.

"So tell me, Althea, what you think about Parke Stockard's murder?" asked Myrtle.

The room fell silent. Althea Hayes and Elaine gaped at her. Jean-Marc and Jack looked bored. Althea straightened up on the settee. "There's nothing to *think* about," she said stiffly. Her look was meant to remind Myrtle that she was sitting in a Very Nice sitting room with many Weathered Antiques Such as the Type that are Handed Down. Murder discussions surely didn't belong in the same room with toile depicting lyrical pastoral scenes.

Myrtle felt a strong urge to squirm under Althea's quelling stare. "Well, you've got to think *something* about it. You were right there at the scene of the crime like I was. And," Myrtle added persuasively, "I'm sure you weren't fond of Parke. Especially considering her spat with Tanner."

Myrtle sucked her breath in sharply at the completely lost look that suddenly consumed Althea's face. Elaine glared at her from across the room and Jean-Marc raised his eyebrows in a rare moment of interest. Just as quickly as it appeared, Althea covered up her emotions. There was still a fear in the back of her eyes. What did Althea know?

"She wasn't the most popular person in town," noted Althea dryly. "But that was no reason for someone to take her life. In *church*!" she stressed with a shake of her snowy-white hair.

"But she was a bull-headed woman. A pretty woman, used to getting her own way. And she wanted us to sell our home so she could turn it into a monster." Althea's bright blue eyes flashed. "She *argued* with Tanner. She acted like she thought he was stupid or crazy not to sell. But this is our *home*. It has been for thirty years. She made Tanner have a heart attack. She made him so mad." Althea looked mad herself.

Elaine stepped in. "I know that must be very painful for you, Althea. Why don't we think about happier things?" she said, with a forceful look at Myrtle.

Elaine racked her brain. "Seasons of the year in France!" she declared. And then, in French, "Jean-Marc, cook us the day of the year in France."

Jean-Marc slapped himself dramatically on the forehead. Then, to the amazement of everyone in the room, Jack said, in French, "Jean-Marc likes Paris in spring." They all gaped at Jack. Then Jean-Marc beamed and shook Jack's hand emphatically while Jack gave a drooling grin.

In Myrtle's mind, once the point of getting any useful information from Althea had passed, she was ready to go home. She tapped her fingers impatiently on the chair arm while Elaine, Althea, Jean-Marc, and even Jack nattered on in various levels of ability in French for another thirty minutes. Myrtle sighed. She would still have to approach Althea about what she was doing in the sanctuary the morning Parke was murdered. But she obviously wasn't going to get anywhere today. Myrtle was vastly relieved when the visit finally drew to an end.

She stood up eagerly, grabbing her cane and starting to tap her way over the oriental rugs to the front door when the doorbell rang. Oh, Lord. She hoped she wasn't about to get stuck at Althea's house. She'd been dying to get over here; now she couldn't wait to leave.

It only got worse when she saw it was Althea's younger sister, Josh's mother, at the door. She stood there in her plain cotton sundress, blinking in confusion at all the visitors and peering anxiously at Althea. "Oh, I didn't know you had company, Althea. Is everything okay?" She spotted Myrtle and said, "Oh, it's you, Myrtle! It's so good to see you. I never seem to get a chance to catch up with you."

And tell me alllll about the wondrous things your son, Wonder Boy, is doing these days. No thanks. Myrtle managed a smile that was more like a grimace. "Hi, Bettie. Nice to see you, too." Now she was in an absolute panic to leave. Elaine didn't appear to be picking up on any of her signals and was instead greeting Bettie and introducing Jean-Marc to her. Even Jack smiled endearingly at Bettie, begging for admiration.

"Jean-Marc," said Bettie, carefully enunciating each word loudly, as if he had a hearing problem instead of a language barrier, "My son works with Myrtle at the newspaper here. The *Bradley Bugle*. Of course, he used to work at a much bigger paper. I know you've heard of it, since it's really an internationally read newspaper. The *New York Times*?"

Jean-Marc nodded his awareness of the paper and somehow hid any irritation he felt at being hollered at from one foot away.

"Yes, he did really well there. Not that he hasn't done well here, either, understand. He's won awards and a huge trophy for the paper."

Myrtle glowered at the mention of the trophy.

"But his father and I were just so happy that he came back here. We'd been having a few health problems, you know. Nothing major, of course. But to have him come back here to help us out was just such a blessing. What a sacrifice, though. Not just for him, leaving his career to come home here. But also for all the readers of the *Times* to have to do without his wonderful articles."

Myrtle had had quite enough of this by now and gave a harrumphing throat-clearing as a sign for Elaine. But Elaine seemed preoccupied with Jack's runny nose. She rifled through her diaper bag for something to wipe it with. Either a tissue or wipe was on the very bottom of the incredibly full bag, or else it wasn't in there at all.

Myrtle noticed there was absolutely no mention of the failed marriage Josh had left behind in New York. She guessed that Bettie wasn't the kind to focus on any of Josh's negatives, if she was even aware that he had any at all. Finally, Elaine found a zipper bag with some wet wipes and swabbed Jack's face and they were out the door a minute later.

On the way back home in the minivan, Myrtle said, "I can't understand what's gotten into Althea! She's not the scary old bat she usually is. She doesn't even seem interested in talking about anything, except France. She's just . . . removed."

A French-accented voice wafted from the backseat. "Eet is the depression."

"Pardon?" asked Myrtle.

Jean-Marc said, "The depression. She withdraws, she doesn't eat. She loses interest. The depression."

Myrtle turned around and looked at Jean-Marc. He had a point. Althea *was* withdrawn. In fact, she was practically hiding.

"She loses her husband. She loses her youth." Jean-Marc gave a Gallic shrug.

Myrtle turned back around to see Elaine's reaction, but Elaine was fumbling in the diaper bag for a snack for a suddenly fussy Jack. Considering she was driving the car at the same time, Myrtle thought that was enough distraction for a while. When Elaine seemed to be paying more attention, Myrtle cleared her throat and said, "You know, Elaine, I really enjoyed going to book club with you last time. There's supposed to be another meeting coming up, right?"

Elaine looked suspicious, but only briefly, as she extended a sippy cup into the depths of the minivan where it disappeared. "Yes, actually, there's a get-together in a couple of days. We couldn't decide which book to read next time, so we were all going to meet and bring books with us that we've enjoyed and decide from there."

"Could you plan on bringing me along? Where is the meeting going to be?"

Elaine smiled. "I won't even have to pick you up, Myrtle. The meeting will be right next door to you at Erma Sherman's house."

Myrtle hissed through her teeth like a snake that has just been stepped on. "Great. I *guess* I enjoyed it enough to put up with Erma. At least she'll have lots of people to torture and I won't be the only victim there."

Chapter Thirteen

Myrtle was apparently Erma's favorite target for persecution. Myrtle had gone through all the precautions, however, peering out her window, making sure that she wasn't the first person to arrive at book club. She couldn't believe it when she saw flocks of white heads entering Erma's house. Didn't they know what they were getting into? Erma should have a sign over her door reading: *Abandon hope all ye who enter here.* Dante would certainly agree that Erma's front door was Purgatory's portal.

A minute later, Myrtle realized the draw. Miles Bradford stood near the appetizer table, clutching a copy of a thick tome that was completely inappropriate for the type of book club he was attending. Myrtle looked at him in sympathy. The poor man should have been told by whoever invited him that it wasn't a *real* book club. Miles looked as if he were expecting an intellectual dialogue and exchange of ideas. The book club widows watched him with predatory eyes. He'd obviously been told it was a co-ed club that discussed real books. Poor soul.

Erma, fortunately, had other victims to torture, so Myrtle wasn't the only target of her long-winded conversations. Although she did spend fifteen minutes at the beginning of the book club meeting slyly conniving to put Myrtle and Miles in the same conversation. ("Myrtle, did I get you a drink? Oh, Miles will get you one—he's right by the drinks table...") Luckily for Erma, Myrtle's patience with this tactic didn't wear out before Erma got bored with it. Myrtle rolled her eyes at Miles who gave her a sympathetic smile. He wore khakis and an open-necked button-down white shirt and was apparently creating quite a stir among the book club ladies. Several of them had coyly cornered him at the food table and were laughing heartily at something he said. Myrtle looked over at him with sympathy. Miles looked ready to bolt.

Kitty Kirk was at the meeting and Myrtle almost didn't recognize her. She'd gotten so used to seeing Kitty in ill-fitting tracksuits and poorly-applied makeup that it was a shock actually to see her looking smart in a black tunic top and khaki capris. She seemed focused today, too. Myrtle wondered if she were on medication. It was such a dramatic change from the last meeting. She even had a book with her. Last time at Tippy's house, Kitty looked as though she didn't realize why she was even there. Myrtle wondered over the sudden change.

Myrtle wandered over to the appetizer table to see why no one seemed to be eating any snacks. The table held a big platter full of watermelon slices and a few red napkins. What kind of hostess served watermelon slices as appetizers? With no plates, either. These watermelons were chock-full of black seeds. Where were you supposed to spit them? Maybe Erma swallowed hers. No wonder she was always complaining about her gross health problems. Having a watermelon growing in your belly would explain a lot.

Erma finally started the meeting. The progression of the meeting was rather chaotic. The idea was for everyone to share whatever recommendation she had for the next month's book club selection, followed by a quick vote for a consensus. The little spiels for the selections quickly grew contentious, however, and everyone ended up speaking at once. Miles, holding *The Brothers Karamazov*, looked bemused and seemed to be searching for an escape hatch. Most of the titles were pretty lightweight reads. Myrtle figured they could compromise by reading several of them before the next meeting. With those kinds of books, it would only take an afternoon.

Elaine leaned over and gave Myrtle a look. "Like dogs fighting over a bone, isn't it? I don't know why Tippy isn't jumping in to impose a little order. She's usually our referee during these crises."

Tippy sat on a sofa near Erma and looked tired and strained. Still chic, thought Myrtle, glancing over her cream-colored suit. But as if she was under a lot of pressure. Always thin, Tippy now looked positively transparent. The blue veins in her arms stood in sharp relief to the rest of her arms and her elegant clothes hung a bit on her frame. She didn't look at all like jumping in and impose order. In fact, Myrtle wondered if Tippy was even paying attention. She seemed miles away. As far away as Miles wanted to be.

As the book club skirmish faded out with Elaine's suggestion that they decide to put *all* the titles on the schedule and read them alphabetically, the members put their differences aside to put away some pastries. Miles took off his wire-rimmed glasses and rubbed his eyes with a tired gesture. He started edging toward the door, looking cautiously around him for predatory widows.

Myrtle really needed to get some information from Althea Hayes and Althea seemed bent on avoiding her at all costs. Could Miles help her out? He had been a great listener and not tried to offer his opinion on everything. He might be willing to help her ask a few questions—and not try to horn in on her investigation. Still she hesitated. He didn't really *know* her and the first time he met her she had just come out of the lake and was waving a cane at him. As far as she knew, he thought she was a kook. But she hadn't gotten that impression from him; he seemed genuinely to be interested in what she was doing. Just when Miles was on the verge of making his escape, Myrtle caught up with him. "Could you try to get something out of Althea Hayes for me?" she muttered through her teeth.

He gave a long-suffering sigh. "Well, you might be the only person to be able to do it!" Myrtle hissed. "Everyone's falling all over themselves trying to talk to you, you know."

He flushed. "I'll give it a try."

"Good. I'm going to try to catch Kitty while she's making sense."

He looked over at Kitty. "Better hurry then." Kitty was staring out a window with an odd expression on her face.

Myrtle sidled up to her. She cleared her throat. Kitty didn't budge. She hummed a little tune from *Showboat*. Kitty didn't glance her way. Myrtle bellowed, "Christopher Columbus!" She had Kitty's attention. Or concern. Or something.

"Kitty dear," Myrtle purred. "You're looking really well." She added in a whispery voice, "Much better than you did at the last book club meeting. Death is always so difficult to deal with, isn't it? Although I've had more experience in dealing with it than most, I'm afraid. Age, you know."

Kitty opened her mouth but no words came out, so Myrtle continued. "How are you doing, dear?"

"Fine, Miss Myrtle. Well, the police don't seem to think I'm that much of a suspect anyway. That's what was bothering me so much last time, you know."

Myrtle thought something else seemed to be bothering her too.

"I hear," Kitty said in a halting voice, "that there were actually two different uh—attackers. That the second blow was the one that killed Parke." She had an odd expression on her face.

Word traveled fast around here. "That's what I understand," said Myrtle.

Kitty spoke slowly. "It was just so funny. You know, that morning Parke was killed."

"What was, dear?"

"The flowers." Myrtle shook her head uncomprehendingly and Kitty said, "There weren't any roses at the church."

Myrtle frowned, trying to decode this cryptic statement, face was a mass of wrinkles. "But there were, Kitty. There were roses all over the sanctuary floor."

Kitty waved her hands in the air with irritation. "Well, enough about all that, anyway." She seemed to be searching her brain for something to say. "Um...what did you think about the meeting today?"

"That it was crazy," answered Myrtle, snorting. "Why Tippy didn't step in and put a stop to all that wrangling is beyond me. Book selection isn't always a free-for-all, is it?"

Kitty gave a short laugh and jammed her hands into the pockets of her khaki capris. "I guess she has a lot on her mind right now."

Myrtle thought that sounded promising. "Why would you think that? Benton's election?"

"No, but the way he trots her out and makes her go to all these clubs keeps her busy enough," said Kitty.

Althea and Miles were still talking. There was a large group standing around Erma that looked in need of rescue. No one appeared to be paying any attention to Kitty and Myrtle.

Kitty seemed relieved that no one appeared to be listening in to their conversation. "I mean, she probably has a lot on her mind because of Parke's murder."

"But Tippy and Benton were here at home. They were each other's alibi," said Myrtle.

Kitty shook her head. "Well, I know for a fact that Tippy wasn't at home. And if *she* wasn't at home, then how does she know that Benton was at home?"

"But she didn't seem to be bothered by any of that at the last book club meeting," Myrtle said.

"Maybe she didn't think Benton could have done it then and was fine with giving him an alibi," said Kitty. "Maybe now she's changed her mind for some reason."

As if she'd found out that Benton was cheating on her and Parke knew about it. "How do you know that Tippy wasn't at home?"

"Oh, she was motoring around in her big Cadillac that morning, looking for greasy food. She called me from her cell phone about the church meeting and said she wasn't going to be able to make the Women of the Church meeting that morning, that she had a terrible headache and was going to just stay home in bed."

Myrtle shrugged. "So?"

"So then I heard a voice say, 'Want some hash browns with that?'" Kitty smiled. "It wasn't Benton's voice."

It sounded like everyone in Bradley, North Carolina, was wandering around town that morning. Myrtle hadn't been able to eliminate anyone for lack of opportunity. Kitty said, "The meeting's breaking up, Miss Myrtle. I'll catch up with you later."

Myrtle looked around her with alarm. Sure enough, the large group of Erma's hostages had broken free of their captor and were streaming out her front door. Myrtle gripped her cane and hurried to the door. Don't look back, she thought. You might turn into a pillar of salt. She heard a nasally voice calling her name behind her and blatantly ignored it, as she escaped from Erma's house and hastened to the refuge of her own home next door.

A few minutes later there was an insistent rap at her door. She cautiously peered through the peephole, expecting to see a distorted version of Erma's rodentesque features on the other side of the door. Instead, she saw Miles' steel-gray hair and irritated face. She opened the door and he stepped inside. Myrtle noticed a cluster of white heads turned in their direction. Biddies. Lord knew what kind of talk was going to be circling around about them.

"Thanks for throwing me to the sharks," he grumbled. "I love the way you beat a path to the door, saving yourself and leaving me in the clutches of Erma and Company." He glowered at her behind his wire-rimmed glasses.

"All's fair in love and war," reminded Myrtle breezily. "Besides, you were supposed to be talking to Althea. Couldn't you have left when she did?"

Miles sighed. "You might have warned me you were sending me on Mission Impossible. Not only was she about as responsive as a rock, but she seemed to get the opinion I was hitting on her. Which she seemed to find deplorable, since she was so recently widowed." He took off his glasses and rubbed his eyes. "In fact, I caught quite a few glares during my so-called conversation with Althea."

"Oh, they were all just jealous you'd gone over to talk to her. Besides, they've already forgotten about your social faux-pas of courting a new widow and are focusing on the fact you bolted into my house as soon as book club was over. You could have just called on the phone, you know," said Myrtle.

Miles sighed in response.

"You didn't find out anything at *all*? You must have picked up *something* from her. You talked to her long enough. I was pumping Kitty for information the same amount of time and found out all kinds of things," said Myrtle.

"Well, that's the difference between your conversation and mine. In my conversation, *I* was doing most of the talking and in yours, it sounds like Kitty was doing most of it. I was just desperate for a topic after a while. Finally got on the topic of her nephew, Josh Tucker. The newspaper guy," he explained.

Myrtle nodded impatiently. "I know who he is."

"She just talked about how he had been such a big shot reporter in New York, then such a devoted son that he left all his success behind to come home and be near his aging parents."

Myrtle rolled her eyes. "Not exactly helpful information, Miles."

"Althea said he wanted to keep churning out award-winning stories so he could still make his parents proud, even though he's really slumming with the paper he's working for."

"The *Bradley Bugle* is a fine paper," retorted Myrtle, stung.

"Sorry, Myrtle. I know you write a column in the *Bugle*. But it's not exactly *The New York Times*, is it?" Getting no answer, he continued, "I know you were put out because Parke's column was getting your column cut back. Maybe Sloan was doing the same thing for Josh Tucker—making him cut back on his stories because of Parke's piece."

"As a matter of fact, I heard from my favorite waitress at Bo's Diner that Sloan *was* cutting Josh's articles. I'd never have suspected that, since Sloan is always so impressed with everything Josh comes up with. Isn't there anything else you found out?"

"Well, no, as you'd have known if you hadn't bolted. About that time Erma Sherman lumbered up, since Althea was discussing what was apparently Erma's favorite topic. She started going on like a lovesick calf, asking all sorts of soppy questions about Josh." Miles plopped down onto Myrtle's sofa and took off his shoes.

"Make yourself comfortable," Myrtle said in a caustic tone.

"Let me catch you up with what I found out from Kitty." Miles listened attentively while she described Kitty's conversation with Tippy on the morning of Parke' murder.

When Myrtle was done, he squinted thoughtfully at Myrtle's ceiling for several minutes. Myrtle was beginning to realize that when Miles was thinking things through he liked to be quiet, so she walked into the kitchen to pour a couple of Coca-Colas.

When she walked back in, Miles said, "So you're thinking that Tippy believes Benton might have killed Parke to keep her from talking about Benton's affair. Or maybe Tippy could have killed Parke. She was out driving around, after all. Half the town was parking at the church for the Women of the Church meeting. She could have run in, hit Parke on the head with the collection plates or candlesticks or whatever, and gone on home."

"I'm not sure that *Tippy* would have killed Parke," answered Myrtle slowly as she handed Miles his drink.

"Why not? She had just as much to lose as Benton. She'd have been humiliated if Benton's affair was common knowledge. It could have made real problems for Benton's political career, which would have damaged Tippy's lifestyle, too."

"I guess. There's something Kitty said that was kind of odd," said Myrtle. "She started going on about flowers at the church. Something about roses not being there. She looked almost worried about it."

"Well, it probably has to do with the fact that she was the one who put the wildflowers in the sanctuary and Parke came in to change them out with one of her *grand arrangements*. Maybe Kitty is still piqued about it."

"Maybe," said Myrtle, "But she didn't sound piqued. And she seemed more concerned that the roses *weren't* there."

"But they *were*. You saw them yourself when you discovered Parke's body. There were roses all over the place you said," said Miles.

Myrtle sighed. "I don't know why I'm trying to make sense out of Kitty Kirk anyway. Even at her best, she's not playing with a full deck."

Miles took a long drink from his Coke. "Better than trying to get information from the secretive Althea." He took his glass into Myrtle's kitchen, putting it in the sink. "I'd better go. The spies are probably out there timing my visit anyhow."

"Well, they have nothing else to think about, you know. Give me a call tomorrow and maybe you can help me decide what I need to focus on next."

There. She'd firmly put him in his sidekick place.

Chapter Fourteen

Myrtle decided that what she needed, really needed, was to host a small dinner party. No, "dinner party" was too extreme. She just needed an excuse to have Red over for dinner and an opportunity to extract information from him. Getting some forensic information would be especially useful. Or even some direction for suspects. Red did love to talk, but usually kept his trap shut when it came to his job. Supper might loosen him up. Besides, she wanted him to properly meet Miles—especially since Red and Elaine lived right across the street from him. She clucked. It was a shame how neighbors didn't meet new neighbors anymore. She would fix that little situation, she decided, benevolently. By the time she picked up the phone to call Elaine, she'd completely convinced herself of her altruistic intentions and nearly forgotten her scheme.

Elaine seemed doubtful at the invitation. "Tonight? What about Jack?"

"Can't Monsieur Marvelous take care of him for just a couple of hours? Jean-Marc? Jack will be sleeping anyway, won't he?"

Elaine had another problem. Myrtle's horrible cooking was legendary to everyone—except Myrtle. How Red had survived, eating her food, for as long as he had was a mystery to her. "That just sounds like a lot of work for you, Myrtle. Can I bring a dish with me?"

"Like some dinner rolls?"

"Or . . . how about a roast?"

"A roast?!"

"Well, I was going to make one for our supper tonight, anyway. I've actually already started on it. Can't I—?"

"No, no, no! Goodness Elaine, you'd think you were never invited to someone's house for supper before. The idea is that *you're* the guest. Bring a bottle of wine or something, but the main course is my job. You have enough going on right now, anyway—time to take it easy and relax. Make your roast another night."

"All right," said Elaine gloomily. Well, she could always tell Red that she'd tried.

"Let's make it a European-style dinner."

Elaine sighed. This was code for "late."

"Maybe 8:00? I'll call Miles."

"So your Pilgrim is pretty nice, hmm?"

"None of that, Elaine. And don't be making little smirky faces at us. We're strictly platonic. I'll see you tonight." She rang off and Elaine was left holding the receiver and wondering how her day had so quickly gotten hijacked.

Miles sounded much more pleased. "That's nice of you, Myrtle. I'd love to come and talk to Red and meet Elaine. The last time I saw Red wasn't exactly conducive to conversation."

"You mean right in the middle of your rescue of a dripping-wet old lady?" Myrtle chuckled. "Should be easier to talk to him this time. Of course, he's a little funny over dinner sometimes. A big man like that you'd think would be able to put away some food. I don't know how he survives—he always picks at his food whenever we're together."

"Probably trying to keep trim for his job."

"Anything you can't eat, Miles? You a vegetarian or anything like that? Allergies?"

"No, I'll eat it all. Just a human garbage disposal."

With those words, Miles Bradford sealed his fate for dinner that night.

Myrtle then called her housekeeper, Puddin. She always had great misgivings when calling Puddin. For one thing, Puddin's husband, Dusty, usually answered the phone. Dusty was Myrtle's yard man and as soon as he heard her voice he'd bellow, "It's too hot to mow!" Then he'd hand the phone over to Puddin who'd decide if she felt like cleaning or not. Puddin's bad back could get thrown out at any time. It was especially contrary when silver needed polishing, toilets scrubbed, or knickknacks dusted.

Puddin sullenly agreed to clean.

Myrtle should have been tipped off that the evening was not going to go as planned when Puddin slouched in two hours late. Puddin's already-evident ill humor worsened at the amount of dust Myrtle expected her to extricate from tables and books. With a dour expression on her dumpy face, she pulled a soiled rag out of her cleaning bucket and resentfully slapped it at the tables. Sunbeams illuminated the dust particles as they flew into the air before settling lazily back again on their original locations.

Watching Puddin dust would only inspire heartburn. Myrtle inspected her recipe and pulled the fish out of the freezer.

Miles reflected later that the evening had started off like any other. There had been little warning of the calamity to come. True, Myrtle had a sour attitude when she greeted Miles at the door, but Miles chalked that up to pre-dinner-party nerves. Although, considered Miles, "greeted" was an exaggeration. Myrtle gave a preoccupied grunt of surprise and wandered back in the direction of the kitchen while working on a roll of plastic wrap. After an unsuccessful attempt to untangle it from its determined clinging to the rest of the roll, she tossed it at the floor with a disgusted sound. Miles stooped, picked it up, and started working patiently at it, glad of something to do since his hostess had forgotten he'd arrived.

Miles wasn't sure exactly what his role should be and cursed the punctuality that had driven him to arrive this early. He milled around Myrtle's small library, pulling out a copy of *The Fountainhead*, not surprised to see comments written in the margins and underlined places and even, in one spot, an exclamation point where the editor for the edition had missed a typo. He took out a well-worn collection of Yeats' poetry and chuckled over some of her exuberant markings. Obviously, he was a favorite of Myrtle's. After a few minutes and since Myrtle still seemed in her own little world, he left the books and walked toward the kitchen. He picked up a small bowl and admired it out loud, hoping to rouse his hostess.

"Umph?" asked Myrtle.

"This is a wonderful porringer. I have never in my life seen one that's brass. Was it yours when you were a baby?" asked Miles politely.

Myrtle shot him a withering stare. "For your information, it's sterling silver. Puddin's back was too thrown out to polish. And no, I am way too young to have eaten from porringers . . . it was my grandmother's. What sort of man knows what porringers are, anyway?"

"I was married for many years, if that's what you're implying," Miles protested mildly.

Elaine and Red arrived after another fifteen or twenty minutes. Miles thought they seemed like nice people, even if Red did appear a little tense. When Myrtle darted back into the kitchen, Red pulled Miles aside. "I want to apologize in advance for all the digestive upset you're about to go through."

Elaine hissed at Red. "It won't be that bad, Red."

"Not bad? Her meat is so leathery we'll be chewing on bits of it hours later. I'll have a mouth full of cracked off fillings from her undercooked vegetables. She'll either take the bread out too early and we'll be eating dough, or she'll forget them and it'll be a brick. This evening has disaster written all over it."

Elaine hushed him as Myrtle hurried back out of the kitchen to pour them all a glass of wine, which Red started downing quickly. Miles could tell that she was trying to weasel some information from Red, but she wasn't pressing too hard. Probably waiting for later in the evening when he might be more relaxed before she really started questioning him.

"So there were probably two perps. Imagine that!"

Red didn't take the bait. "Perps. You watching *Law and Order* again, Mama?"

The red flag first went up when Red started sniffing the air and not in an enjoying-the-aroma kind of way. "*What* is that smell? Like something dead." Without waiting for an answer from his affronted mother, he strode into Myrtle's kitchen with Miles behind him and yanked open the oven door. "Oh, ugh!"

Miles took a wild guess that the entrée had swum in fresh or salt water in its former life. He could tell mainly by the smell instead of by looking at the charred mess. Not only was it charred, it was rapidly becoming charcoal, judging from the flames rising out of the oven. Red cursed, pulled on some oven mitts, and jerked out the food. He pulled off a dish towel and beat the fish with it until the fire went out. The smoke billowing from the oven set off Myrtle's smoke detector, which alerted the guests with a shrill, angry sound. Miles opened the kitchen windows and tried fanning the smoke out with a tray. He ignored the face of Erma Sherman, staring goggle-eyed at him from a window next door.

"Guess the butter must have started a fire," muttered Myrtle.

"Might've helped if you'd put the fish in a Pyrex instead of just on the tinfoil. Butter splattered all over the bottom of the oven, Mama."

Myrtle sputtered indignantly, "Well, it's blackened tilapia, Red. Don't you ever go to restaurants?"

"Not to places that serve food like this! Because they wouldn't be open, they'd be shut down by the Board of Health."

Elaine didn't say anything, but her pretty features were contorted as if she were choking back a laugh. Miles' smile looked more like clenched teeth. He was definitely trying to have a good time, thought Elaine. She really should have warned him what he was getting into. She said, "It looks like Myrtle has put together a delicious salad. Want me to help you put it out on the table?"

Red was already lifting lids off pots on the stove and suspiciously peering inside them. "Weren't you supposed to put some water in with your green beans, Mama?"

"I did!"

"Sure doesn't look that way. They're little desiccated logs." He switched off the knob and took the pot off the stove, dumping the contents in the trashcan. Red looked cautiously around the kitchen as though decomposing food might leap out at him from the shadows. "Anything else I should know about?"

"No, that was pretty much the whole menu," Myrtle growled, glaring at Red as if the entire fiasco was his fault. He opened his mouth to argue with her and closed it when his cell phone went off.

"Bradley Police," he said into the phone. He listened for a minute, then used a placating voice Myrtle recognized. "Well, that's not really long enough to declare someone 'missing,' Miz Hall." He listened again for a minute. "No, really—ten minutes late for an event does not mean a person has vanished." More listening. "All right. I'll go check on her."

Red hung up the phone and rubbed his eyes. "Miz Hall says that Kitty Kirk is ten minutes late to meet her for a movie. I'm supposed to go make sure she's all right." He shrugged at Miles. "Welcome to small town life."

Myrtle said, "Well ordinarily I'd say that Lucia Hall was kind of batty, but Kitty Kirk is one of those people who lives by the clock, Red. You could set your watch by her. Ten minutes late to something is a bad sign."

"Sorry to break up the party, Mama. Y'all enjoy dinner." He murmured to Elaine, "Saved by the bell."

Myrtle said, "Oh Red! Before you go, remember you promised to program my new cell phone for me. The default ringtone is just awful. It plays the "Star Spangled Banner" and scares the fool out of me."

Red grumbled, "All right, all right," and stepped into the back bedroom with her phone. A few minutes later he returned to the kitchen and laid the phone on the counter. "Nice phone, Mama," he said. "It's got all the bells and whistles."

"I know. It's the bells and whistles that give me all the trouble. All I really want is to make and answer phone calls."

"I'll show you how to program some numbers in, Myrtle. The one-touch dialing is really cool," said Elaine. She took the phone and programmed in some of Myrtle's most-called numbers while Red grabbed his keys and left. Looking back, Myrtle later realized his smirk should have warned her that Red had been up to something.

After Elaine showed Myrtle how to use the one-touch dialing, Myrtle said to Miles, "Well, that's enough technology for me today. Let's move on to supper. I'm glad you said you have such a healthy appetite, Miles, since we have some extra food with Red gone."

Elaine smiled sympathetically at Miles. "I'll open up more wine."

But Elaine's cell phone rang before she picked up the corkscrew. It was Jean-Marc, calling because Jack was crying and wouldn't stop. "I'm so sorry, Myrtle. I guess the evening must be cursed. Jack is probably just teething, but his ears sometimes bother him when his gums hurt, too. It's awful to just hear him cry. Must be driving poor Jean-Marc crazy—I'd better go." Myrtle turned away to close the kitchen windows and Elaine whispered to Miles, "Sorry. I should have warned you about Myrtle's cooking."

With that, Myrtle and Miles and a big salad were left in the room. Myrtle looked cross. "So much for getting information from Red."

Miles figured this was a situation that called for some tact. "You were saying, though, that being ten minutes missing was a big deal for Kitty Kirk?"

"She's just one of those clock-watchers. Has conniptions if she's a minute late to something." Myrtle pulled out the wine cork and poured a couple of glasses. "I wonder how long she really *has* been gone. Let's call her house."

Kitty's husband Tiny answered the phone. "Nope. Haven't seen her," he said.

"Haven't seen her since when? I'm—ah—trying to find out about the Women of the Church meeting coming up."

There was an irritated sigh on the other end of the line. "Don't really know, Miss Myrtle. She left this morning when I was getting ready for work. A *long* day at work. Kitty was going to see a movie tonight with Lucia Hall."

"I believe she was late getting over there."

"She was *not*."

"I beg your pardon—you've heard from her? She ended up making it over to Lucia's house?"

"I've not heard a word. But Kitty would *never* be late. Not ever." He sounded quite offended by the very idea.

Myrtle decided not to fill him in on Kitty's absence. He'd probably just snap at her. She thanked him and he'd hung up before she'd said goodbye.

"Well, that went nowhere," she told Miles.

"He obviously doesn't think she's missing."

"No, Tiny thinks she's at a movie with Lucia." Myrtle tapped her wine glass on the table and Miles winced as the sloshing red wine dripped onto her white tablecloth.

"Let's suppose she really is missing. It's not an unreasonable idea, considering what we know about her." Myrtle took a long sip of her wine.

"Okay," said Miles. "So she's missing. Why would she be missing?"

"Maybe she knows something," mused Myrtle. "In fact, we know she knew something because she told me about it. She knew that Tippy Chalmers was out driving around instead of at home, as she'd claimed. Kitty knew that neither Benton's nor Tippy's alibi was legitimate."

Miles considered it. "Even so, it seems like a mighty flimsy reason for killing someone. You're saying that she confronted Tippy or Benton with her information and that one of them did her in?"

"Why not? One of them had murdered once already. They would need to shut Kitty up if they had any hope of getting away with the crime. Let's say Kitty was really worried about what she knew. She arranged to meet with Tippy or Benton to talk about it."

Miles squinted doubtfully. "I don't know, Myrtle. Seems like she would just pick up the phone and make a call. Why all the cloak and dagger stuff?"

Stumped, Myrtle tapped her wine glass again. Then she perked up and said, "Maybe she wanted to blackmail them!" Miles snorted and Myrtle said, "No, really! Think about it—she's stuck at home with Tiny, who doesn't even care whether she's missing or not. She's never had any money of her own, never worked. No independence. Her son is finally out of the house—maybe she's ready to spread her wings and have a little freedom. The Chambers family has plenty of money—and enough at stake to make a good mark for her."

Miles sipped his wine. "Could be. So you're thinking she arranged to meet them somewhere and instead of paying out, they did her in?"

Myrtle looked solemn. "Poor Kitty."

"We don't even know that she's dead yet, Myrtle. Where do you think she'd have set up this little rendezvous? Where are all the deserted places?"

"The rural highway near Crazy Dan, the old quarry, the playground on the other side of town (depending on the time of day) . . . or maybe the cemetery." Myrtle mulled it over. "I don't see Kitty getting too far away. She hasn't left town a day in her life, I don't think. No, she'd want to stay in familiar territory. She has a family plot at Rose Hill." She reached over and grabbed Miles' sleeve, nearly causing him to spill his wine, too. "Let's go there."

He gaped at her. "To the cemetery?" It was nearly 9:00.

"You've got a car. It won't take long to just drive through there."

"And what are we going to tell Red if we find anything?"

"We'll just make it up as we go along, Miles. 'Nice night for a drive through the cemetery' or something like that. Come on, let's go!"

Miles looked wistfully at the large bowl of salad (even though the lettuce leaves were wilting under the large amount of Italian dressing poured on top.) and followed Myrtle out the door.

The cemetery was about a ten-minute drive from the center of town. It had been Bradley's premier burial spot for the past 150 years with old, moss-covered tombstones next to brand-new markers. There were old gates surrounding ancient family plots, rows of cement crosses, and old white oak trees towering over the graves as if watching the proceedings. Kudzu had recently taken a stranglehold over an older section of the cemetery and engulfed many trees, making them look like green, leafy ghosts.

"Don't you think," Miles asked slowly, "that this is an odd place for a person to arrange to meet a murderer? After all, Parke's grave is here."

"Well, I don't think the murderer really has too many compunctions about that. He was able to murder Parke in cold blood, after all. Probably not the superstitious type."

They drove in silence for a minute. The narrow, paved road wound through the graves. When they reached an older part of the cemetery with tilting, mossy gravestones and heavier tree cover, Myrtle suddenly cried out. "What's that up ahead?"

There was a dark lump on a grave that looked people-sized. Miles moved his car so that the headlights shone on the figure. "It's a body," he said grimly.

Chapter Fifteen

Kitty's compact car was parked nearby. Myrtle moved to open the door and Miles's arm shot out to stop her. "We need to call Red on this one. The murderer still could be lurking around. And who knows what kind of clues we could be tampering with if we trample in there?"

"I don't *plan* on trampling, Miles. But I do think we have a responsibility to see if Kitty—or whoever it is—is breathing. We could help her. I'll get right back in the car. For heaven's sake, no one's going to attack me with your headlights shining like a spotlight. They'd be nuts."

"They must *be* nuts, Myrtle."

"I'll tread softly."

Myrtle grasped her cane and moved cautiously forward. She wanted to see clues herself and had no intention of destroying anything. The ground was uneven and rocky, which caused her to move even more carefully. When Myrtle got within several feet of the figure, she saw that it was Kitty Kirk and that there was no question that she was dead from a blow to the head. A cement cross that must have broken off a tombstone was lying next to her. Standing very still, Myrtle also noticed, in the glare of the headlights, something out of the corner of her eye. Leaning forward on her cane, she peered at the object on the ground, then walked to the car where Miles was already talking on his cell phone. She opened her mouth to speak and Miles held up a hand.

"That's right, Red." He winced a little and held the phone away from his ear. "No, you didn't misunderstand me. Right. No, she's right here in the car with me. I'll see you in a minute."

"Sounds like someone wasn't a happy camper?" asked Myrtle with a smirk.

Miles leaned back onto the headrest. "You could say that. I don't think he was excited to have another murdered body on his watch and he was especially disturbed at having his mother discover the body—again."

"At least we're helping him out. An extra set of eyes."

Miles was about to answer that he didn't think Red viewed it that way when Myrtle waved him quiet. "Let me tell you what I found, Miles. Uh—besides poor Kitty, of course. I also saw a checkbook on the ground ... Cecil Stockard's checkbook." Her voice was high with excitement.

"Cecil?"

Myrtle nodded impatiently. "Yes, we were all wrong, Miles, all wrong. We should have been thinking about Cecil all along. He was the one who gambled, who used and sold drugs. He was the one who needed money and probably thought his mom's death would solve all his financial problems."

Miles frowned. "But wouldn't he know the way the will was set up? That his sister and charities would be getting the bulk of her money?"

"Why would he? He had every right to assume that his mother would remember him in her will."

"But you told me when you talked with Cecil at the funeral that he claimed he knew that his mother planned to basically write him out of her will. And that she was a lot more useful to him alive than dead."

"Well, maybe he was just saying that to throw me off track. The fact is, his checkbook at the scene of a crime. I guess we were right—Kitty did have some information and intended to blackmail the murderer to get some money. And Kitty didn't have any love for Cecil anyway—he was the one that introduced her son to drugs, remember? So she would really have wanted to stick it to him. Rattle his cage a little. He probably figured she'd be holding it over him her whole life—and decided to end it prematurely," said Myrtle.

Miles nodded his head slowly. "It does make sense. But Cecil wouldn't have been able to pay Kitty anything; he was broke."

"But Kitty wouldn't have known that. She didn't exactly call up Cecil for social chats. She'd have thought he had a big chunk of Parke's fortune and that he owed it to her to share. And Cecil would have almost *had* to have killed Kitty—he knew he couldn't possibly pay her demands either now or over time."

Headlights were now visible as a white police car snaked through the winding road. The car came to a stop and Red and Detective Lieutenant Perkins stepped out. Perkins, flashlight in hand, walked over to the body on the grave and Red walked over to Miles's car. Miles noticed that Myrtle had adopted a demure expression. Or as demure as a tall, big-boned lady could appear.

Red opened the passenger side door and stood looking at his mother with his eyebrows up questioningly. "Are you a professional victim-finder now, Mama?"

Myrtle coughed delicately. "Miles and I thought it would be a nice night to go out for a drive. You know, a full stomach, looking for something relaxing to do."

"Stop right there. I can already tell you're fibbing. There's no way you could possibly have a full stomach after tonight's culinary disaster unless you raided your pantry for cereal and Pop Tarts. And a nice night for a drive through the cemetery? Do I need to drive a stake through your heart?"

"At least I'm doing you a favor by finding Kitty Kirk before too much time has gone by. Maybe you can get some forensic information easier than you would have been able to tomorrow or whenever she would have been found." She gestured over to where Perkins was canvassing the ground with his high-beam flashlight. "I can also tell you that he's about to discover Cecil Stockard's checkbook not too far from Kitty's body," said Myrtle, her voice rising victoriously. "Looks like she was trying to blackmail him for killing his mother. He came equipped with his checkbook, then decided to kill Kitty instead of paying out to her for years. Case solved."

Red shook his salt-and red-pepper head. "Case unsolved. Cecil Stockard has been incarcerated all day in Bradley's friendly neighborhood jail cell for drunk driving."

Myrtle's face fell. "All day?"

Red nodded. "Since 5:00 this morning when he was driving home totally smashed."

Miles said thoughtfully, "So that means that somebody set him up. Not knowing he would have an iron-clad alibi." Myrtle bobbed her head in excitement.

"Or else," Red said dryly, "he just dropped his checkbook when he was in the cemetery for his mother's funeral."

Myrtle grated, "His mother's plot is clear on the other side of the cemetery. I doubt he wanders through the graveyard for his health."

"But he might meet up with 'business associates' here for drug deals. Could be a very simple explanation."

There was something still bothering Myrtle, niggling in the back of her mind. Something about Cecil. She searched her memory, then gave up. Maybe it would come to her later.

Red shut Myrtle's door soundly and joined Perkins. Myrtle saw Red scan the ground, then point out the checkbook to Perkins and gesture towards his mother. "I still think somebody tried to incriminate Cecil for Kitty's murder. Which means this murder was carefully planned. Kitty would have called the murderer up, threatening exposure or blackmail. The murderer arranged to meet her here sometime today—it wouldn't have even had to be dark because the cemetery is usually deserted. He picks up part of a broken tombstone, clobbers Kitty over the head, and plants evidence to implicate Cecil Stockard. It seems pretty well thought-out. Someone was desperate not to be discovered."

Miles' stomach growled and he glanced at his watch. It was 9:45 and still no sign of a meal. He watched as Red and Perkins trained their flashlights on some tire tracks. "I guess they'll want to ask us some questions?" he asked gloomily.

"I'm sure they will. After all, our deductions led to the discovery of Kitty's body." Myrtle sighed sadly. "I do feel bad about Kitty. She really hasn't had a very easy life between her mediocre marriage and her son's drug problems. Blackmailing a murderer was a very stupid thing to do, but I guess she saw it as a way to get a little money of her own and improve her life. She didn't deserve this."

Miles was not thinking very charitably about Kitty Kirk as he was beginning to associate her with his rumbling stomach. "At least they can ask us a few questions now and let us go back home. I'm starving."

Myrtle absently tapped her fingers on the dashboard. "Hold on. I'm thinking." She reached over and pulled Miles' sleeve. "What if we make some excuse and have them question us at the station?"

"Why would we do that?" groaned Miles, wondering if this night was ever going to end.

"The cells are right there at the station. Sort of like Mayberry. If we can get over there, we can maybe stick our head in the jail section and ask Cecil a couple of questions."

Sarcasm was bubbling up inside Miles at the thought of more delay. "Oh, I just bet that Red and Perkins will be delighted to have us question Cecil. What exactly are they supposed to be doing in the meantime while we're following this line of inquiry?"

Myrtle ignored his tone. "We'll think of something. Maybe we'll send them out for food or something."

By this time a forensics truck was pulling up and a team was already jumping out and setting up crime tape around the scene.

With all the activity and police vehicles arriving, Miles was looking even more uncomfortable by the minute. When Red walked by the car, Miles rolled down his window and called, "Shouldn't Myrtle and I get out of the way? Should I drive somewhere else?"

Red answered, "You are kind of in the middle of everything, but I do need to get a statement from you."

Myrtle leaned over Miles and asked, "Why don't we go down to the station?"

Red considered this. "I could stand to pick up some things from there. I didn't realize when I left your house that I'd be gone this long. Okay, just follow me over to the station. It should only take a minute. I've got other things to do—like informing Kitty's husband."

Myrtle could only imagine how that would go. Red would probably tell Tiny Kirk that Kitty was dead and he'd answer, "She is *not*!" He appeared to be very indignant over any of Kitty's perceived shortcomings. He'd likely view death as the ultimate character flaw.

The drive to the station took only minutes and soon Miles and Myrtle were sinking into the vinyl station sofas with the broken springs and Red sat with his pen poised, waiting for their story. Myrtle was stalling. It was all going too quickly for her plan. And there were too many policemen going in and out of the station. She said, "Red, I'm famished. Could you run get me some food right quick before we go over this? I'm starting to feel kind of sick."

Red frowned and opened his mouth to give her a piece of his mind when Miles quietly added, "Actually, I'm pretty hungry myself, Red. I hate to cause you anymore problems tonight, but don't *you* need supper, too, before you keep working? If memory serves, you were at the same dinner party I was tonight."

"And there's that fast food place around the corner that's open until 2:00," offered Myrtle. She blinked innocently at him as if thinking she'd given a very helpful suggestion.

"I thought you'd gone for a nice ride in the cemetery on your full stomach," Red reminded her sourly and he was rewarded with a blush from Myrtle. "Okay. I'll pick something up real quick and we can eat while I get your statements from you. Just stay put," he said firmly, "and don't go finding any more bodies." He took his keys out of his pocket and walked out the door.

Myrtle grabbed her cane and struggled to her feet. "Let's get moving before somebody else comes through the revolving door. You'd think the whole universe was centered around the Bradley Police Department tonight."

The small police station featured a door leading to Red's office on one side of the lobby and a metal, swinging door leading to a series of six jail cells on the other side. The Bradley jail usually served as a holding tank for more serious offenders until they could be transferred elsewhere, or as a place for DUIs to sober up. Such was the case tonight with Cecil Stockard.

Cecil sat on the cot in the cell. His black hair hung greasily in his face and he didn't look like he'd shaved in at least a day. Myrtle doubted he smelled minty fresh and stayed far enough back to ensure she wouldn't find out. He looked up when they walked through and smirked at them. His voice was slurred and Myrtle wondered if he could possibly still be drunk after so many hours behind bars, or if he were just tired. "Miss Meddlesome Myrtle and friend. How nice to see you. I'd offer you some refreshments," he waved a hand around, "but as you can see, there's not much in the way of snacks here."

"Ah...sorry to see you here in such circumstances, Cecil."

He nodded, lank hair falling into his eyes. He pushed it back with a grubby hand. "And you're sharing these aforementioned circumstances for some reason?"

Myrtle took a deep breath. "Because we discovered Kitty Kirk's murdered body. We're here to give our statement." She watched Cecil's features carefully and saw what looked like genuine surprise pass across his face. "Really. Kitty Kirk?" He looked puzzled, as if he couldn't connect Kitty Kirk with a violent death—as if he knew far better candidates for such a fate.

Miles coughed. "And we also found your checkbook. At the scene of the crime."

A crimson flush spread over Cecil's face and his eyes glittered with rage. "I haven't been anywhere near the woman. And I've been rotting in this dungeon all day long. I mean *all* day." His eyes flicked around the cell. "Somebody tried to set me up. My checkbook has been lost at least a week—someone must have swiped it and put it there."

Miles poked Myrtle. "We'd better get out to the lobby, Myrtle."

"Can't be seen fraternizing with the criminal, hmm?" jeered Cecil as they beat a hasty retreat. They had just taken their seats in the lobby when Red came through the door bearing a large white bag with grease dripping through.

"Hey," said Red, "that took a little longer than I planned. Here's your food...Miles, I super-sized yours, because I figured you'd be starving by now. Let me just jot down your statement and I'll eat mine on the road." With that, he wrote their story down, shaking his head from time to time. Finally he said, "Okay, I think that's it. You can go on home now." He left, chomping down huge gulps of a cheeseburger as he went. Passing him on the way into the station were several officers from the state police.

"Wanna blow this joint?" Miles gritted through his teeth in what he fondly imagined was a realistic film noir manner.

Myrtle, still munching on French fries, said, "Sure. Oh, can you run by Nathaniel Gluck's house on the way home?"

Miles, beginning to regret that he still had a valid driver's license, sighed. "The minister's? Why? No—never mind. I don't want to know."

Nathaniel Gluck greeted them at the front door. He was wearing a long nightshirt, which Myrtle thought had gone out of fashion in the 1950s. His spindly arms and legs stuck out of the bottom of the nightshirt like a stick person and he bore a striking resemblance to Ichabod Crane. Or Wee Willie Winkie. And there was something else ... Myrtle wrinkled her nose. "You smoke!" she barked in surprise.

Nathaniel turned bright red. Poor guy, thought Miles, probably trying to sneak in a last cigarette of the day before turning in. Caught in the act by Myrtle "The Nose" Clover.

"I'm trying to break the habit," Nathaniel said, gathering his dignity around him.

Myrtle was completely put out. Her main clue from Parke's murder scene had turned into a red herring. She'd obviously just smelled smoke from Nathaniel's clothing in the sanctuary. She tried to remember her train of thought.

Miles stepped in, trying to keep the poor minister from thinking that an anti-smoking committee had arrived on his front porch. "The reason we're here," he glanced over to Myrtle for affirmation because he really had no idea exactly why they *were* there, "is because Kitty Kirk has been murdered." As the minister gaped at them, Myrtle stepped in, "And Red is getting ready to go notify Tiny Kirk. You might want to run by there. And since it was Kitty, and knowing what a big role she played at the church, I thought you'd want to hear about it."

Nathaniel nodded. "Thanks for letting me know, Miss Myrtle."

Possessing a natural killer instinct, Myrtle realized this was the perfect opportunity to catch him off-guard. She quickly added, "One more thing that's been on my mind for a while. You really jumped to Althea's defense when she showed up at the sanctuary the morning of Parke's murder. Could you tell me why that was?"

The minister gave Myrtle a stern look. "I certainly will not, Miss Myrtle. That's confidential." He gently but firmly closed the front door behind him to get dressed.

Finally, Miles and Myrtle were on their way back home. Myrtle was quiet on the short drive, planning her suspect interviews. Miles, no longer obsessed with the vacant nature of his stomach, felt sleepy and was eager to divest himself from his new friend, at least temporarily. He'd never dreamed that retiring to a small town would end up being so exciting.

Chapter Sixteen

The list of suspects seemed to be dwindling. Kitty Kirk could still have killed Parke Stockard, but it made more sense that she was killed because someone *else* was the murderer and she'd known about it. Cecil Stockard could have killed his mother, but it seemed unlikely since he'd had an iron-clad alibi for Kitty's murder and it appeared the two murders were linked. Which meant the suspects Myrtle still needed to talk to were Benton and Tippy Chambers, Josh Tucker, and Althea Hayes.

She was just figuring out how to manipulate a time to talk to each of them when Myrtle's doorbell rang. She frowned and checked her kitchen wall clock. 7:00 a.m. She picked up her cane and walked over to the front door, peeking out through the sheer curtains at the window next to the door. She saw Josh Tucker standing out there and figured that Wonder Boy was all ready to interview her for the big story. Hopefully he wouldn't use too many adjectives in his article. Myrtle could just see it now: *Myrtle Clover, appearing wan and wearing a tatty-looking polyester robe, recounted her harrowing story.*

She opened the door and saw Josh glance over her appearance and start to apologize for coming over so early. She cut him off: "It's no problem, Josh. I'm just getting a late start to my day. Come on in and have some coffee with me. I guess you're wanting a first-hand account of what happened last night? Word spread fast, but that's pretty typical."

They settled into Myrtle's kitchen. Although it was the scene of many culinary disasters, its cheeriness made it her favorite room. Red checked curtains hung at the windows, the walls were a sunny yellow, and Myrtle had a set of soup-bowl-sized coffee cups in improbably wild colors into which she poured hefty helpings of java for them both.

Myrtle told the story of the drive to the cemetery the night before, conveniently leaving out the tale of the dinner party that had led to the outing (and hoping that the remains of the food weren't smelling up the space too much). She hadn't had a chance to take out the garbage yet.

When she wrapped up the story, Josh looked at her admiringly. She had a suspicious moment when she wondered if he were trying to butter her up to get more information out of her. He was nuts if he thought she was going to share her clues and insights with him so he could get the credit for solving the case. He said, "So by following your gut instincts, you ended up discovering Kitty Kirk's body in the cemetery. Your intuition is really beating the police department's, Miss Myrtle. And it sounds like you're very perceptive, too. Did you—ah—uncover any clues as to the murderer while you were there?"

Myrtle preened at the praise, but wasn't tricked into giving away any information. "Well, that's Red's job though, isn't it? I'm sure they've canvassed the area and if there's anything to be found, they found it."

Josh took a long swig of his coffee. "Off the record, Miss Myrtle," (which set the alarm bells off in Myrtle's head since reporters were never really off-record), "Who do you think is behind all this? Bradley, North Carolina, doesn't exactly have a real crime problem. Two murders in about as many weeks is almost unbelievable."

Myrtle nodded. "It hasn't exactly been a normal couple of weeks around here, has it? I can't say I have any idea what has suddenly introduced this element into the town, Josh."

"It almost seems," Josh said in a gossipy voice, "that it came in with some newcomers to town." He looked meaningfully at her.

"If you mean did all this start with Parke's arrival to town, I'd have to agree with you. She had a way of stirring things up." Myrtle watched with interest as Josh blushed. He must have had some kind of crush on Parke. But then, she was a gorgeous and accomplished woman. Maybe it was to be expected.

"And hasn't Cecil Stockard been an instigator, too?" Josh asked innocently. He was obviously fishing for the hot quote. Myrtle wasn't forgetting that he had his reporter hat on. He wasn't just sitting in her kitchen having a neighborly cup of coffee with her, she reminded herself.

Myrtle didn't answer and Josh tried again. "I mean, he seems to end up on the wrong side of the law sometimes, doesn't he? There were always allegations of drug use, right? And some talk of online gambling?"

Figuring he'd find out soon enough anyway, Myrtle said, "That's all true, Josh. But Cecil Stockard was in the Bradley jail during the murder yesterday." Josh sat back in the wooden chair with surprise and Myrtle continued, "Yes. For DUI. So he's out of the picture for Kitty's murder anyway. I know you're trying to do some reporting, Josh, but you ought to be more careful where you're prying. It could be very dangerous."

Josh looked disappointed. "I guess I could put a blurb about his arrest in the crime report, anyway." He finished up with his coffee and quickly made his departure to write up his story. His phone rang as he was leaving and Myrtle followed him outside, on the pretense of watering her potted geraniums.

"And what was your reaction when you heard about Kitty Kirk's death?" Josh was asking. He listened and made some notes on a pad as he walked slowly around the gnomes in the front yard. Myrtle rolled her eyes. He was obviously going for the gut responses and ignoring the factual side of the story. "And were you surprised to hear she'd been murdered, Ms. Sherman?" Great. And obviously playing on Erma's infatuation with him and her general sense of melodrama to help him with his story.

Myrtle watched him get in his car and drive off. She just couldn't see Josh as a possible suspect. She'd originally included him on her list because he'd sounded as apprehensive about Parke's conquering column as she'd been. Now she just wondered if he was commiserating with her out of kindness. And Josh appeared to have had a crush on Parke. He turned bright red whenever her name was mentioned.

At least she hadn't had to go out of her way to find Josh to talk to him. Now she just had to go down the list and talk to the rest of her suspects. She started thinking about Tippy Chambers. Too bad book club wouldn't meet until next month.

Who'd have guessed she'd be so eagerly waiting for book club? Myrtle shook her head in amazement.

She looked over at her calendar. There was a Women of the Church meeting scheduled for 11:00 at the church hall. She beamed. Maybe it was good that Red had signed her up for all that garbage. It gave her the perfect chance to talk to Tippy Chambers. She got dressed.

The church was a fairly easy walk from her house. Luckily it was a nice day, even if it was already hot as the hinges. The seer-sucker suit she was wearing stuck to her a little as she made her way to the church, thumping with her cane as she went.

She was rewarded for her vigilance by the sight of Benton Chambers talking with Tippy in the church parking lot. As Myrtle walked up to them, Tippy started walking into the church. Benton saw Myrtle and moved toward his car. Was he running away from her? Pleased as Myrtle was by the idea, she decided he must actually be headed back to work. She called out to him: "Yoo-hoo! Benton?"

He stiffened a bit, then turned around with a gracious, politician smile covering his face. "Why, Miss Myrtle! How are you doing today, ma'am? Isn't it a nice day?"

"Well, I guess so. A little on the hot side maybe. I was wondering if you'd heard the news? About Kitty Kirk?"

He must have heard something, because an odd expression crept over his face and he plunged his hand into his suit pocket. "Sorry, Miss Myrtle. I've got a phone call."

"I didn't hear it ring," she said suspiciously.

"Had it on 'vibrate,'" he said, hitting a button on the phone and eagerly saying, "Hello?" as he walked to his BMW. *BM-dubyer,* thought Myrtle, remembering Crazy Dan.

Myrtle rooted around in her large pocketbook for her own phone. She wanted to tell Elaine about Benton's reaction and see if she thought it seemed suspicious, too.

She pulled out her phone, then put it back as soon as she'd gotten it. What was the use of calling Elaine? She knew exactly what would happen. Myrtle would ask Elaine if she thought Benton Chambers was evasive for leaping all over his cell phone. In the background, Jack would be howling over a dropped Fruit Loop, Red would be fussing over a broken laptop computer, Jean-Marc would be muttering in sullen French. Elaine would pretend to listen, then she'd answer, "Yes, I do like chamber music. But not in church" or some such nonsense before she'd quickly get off the phone. No, she was going to have to depend on herself more for this case. Elaine had gone from burned-out mommy to amateur zookeeper.

Myrtle puzzled over her transformation from sought-after friend of years past to the lonelier—self-reliant, she corrected—person she was now. Then she smiled. She'd call Miles up a little later and bounce the idea off him. With that settled in her mind, she made her way into the church hall where most of the Women of the Church were already waiting for the meeting to begin. Myrtle saw that Tippy Chambers, wearing a bright red suit, had a free seat next to her. Myrtle quickly sat down, turning immediately to talk to Tippy. The meeting started right away, though, stymieing her efforts.

Myrtle's thoughts wandered as the meeting's chairwoman had the secretary read the minutes from the last meeting. Meetings were the bane of her existence and she avoided them whenever possible. Which was a major reason why she hadn't signed up for Women of the Church herself. The secretary seemed to drone on and on. The air conditioner in the church hall was loud, too, contributing to the white noise effect. Myrtle later supposed that she had drifted off to sleep in her chair. There was really no other explanation how she ended up with her head snuggled onto Tippy Chambers' shoulder.

She sat up and looked apologetically at Tippy, who gave her a polite, if slightly icy, smile. Myrtle guessed that Tippy didn't have too many people in her life who dared to wrinkle her suits or who fell asleep on them. Myrtle willed herself to stay awake, pinching her arm surreptitiously. The meeting hadn't gotten any more exciting while she'd been asleep and several members were now arguing monotonously over some church business. As far as Myrtle could tell, they were covering the same material over and over again without adding any new suggestions or ideas.

She glanced over at Tippy to see if she was as bored with the meeting as Myrtle was. The problem with Tippy, she decided, was that she was just so darn professional in her volunteering. So gung-ho, so interested. It just didn't seem right, Myrtle thought maliciously, that Tippy should be as engrossed by this ridiculous meeting. And her involvement in the proceedings would likely extend after the meeting, with Tippy going up to discuss further some absurdity raised during the assembly. No, this was the perfect time to talk to Tippy.

Myrtle adopted her most old lady-esque demeanor and tugged at Tippy's suit sleeve. Tippy gave her a long-suffering look, but having been raised to always respect her elders, obediently leaned over to listen to Myrtle's stage whispers.

"Did you hear about Kitty Kirk?" Myrtle asked.

Tippy looked at her pityingly. "Yes, we were talking about it while you were asleep. We're trying to decide on an appropriate memorial at the church since Kitty was so involved here."

Myrtle was horrified that she'd missed the only interesting part of the meeting. "Did they discuss what happened to her?"

"No, we just said a prayer for her family, organized a sign-up to bring food over to them, and discussed the possible memorials." Tippy pointedly trained her eyes back to the front of the church hall.

"It was murder, you know," said Myrtle in what she fondly considered an undertone.

A hard glint appeared in Tippy's green eyes as she cut them across to look at Myrtle. "I heard that. Poor Kitty."

"It's so terrible to think," said Myrtle in her best frail old lady manner, "that when I was spending my day preparing for a small dinner party, poor Kitty was suffering." She paused. "What were you doing when poor Kitty was being murdered?"

Tippy's breath hissed out. "Well, I have no idea, Miss Myrtle. I really don't know anything about the murder. I had many different meetings to attend yesterday, so was running around town all day getting ready for garden club, altar guild, and the historical society."

"And Benton was, too?" asked Myrtle. She tried to appear merely conversational, but Tippy was definitely looking suspicious. "Yes, Benton was, too. The campaign is in full-swing, you know."

Suddenly, Red's voice blared out, "ARE YOU TRYING TO KILL ME?" Myrtle whirled around but didn't see him anywhere. Everyone at the meeting turned to stare as the belligerent question repeated. Myrtle realized that Red's voice seemed to be coming from her voluminous pocketbook. Tippy shot her a withering be-quiet!-look. Myrtle snatched up her handbag and cane and hurried to the door. That Red. When he programmed her new cell phone the night of the dinner party, he'd recorded a voice-tone that would "ring" whenever someone called her. She fumbled with the phone, trying unsuccessfully to change it back to a regular ringtone or even to turn the ring volume down. He'd really fixed her wagon this time. She gave up messing with the phone settings and stuck the phone inside a wad of tissues, deep down in her pocketbook.

"Mama needs another project," growled Red as he stomped through the police station door. Perkins was holding a file and raised a questioning eyebrow.

"I just drove past the church and saw her harassing Benton Chambers, trying to muscle information out of him. She's really going to get herself killed."

"So she needs another red herring? I guess she didn't figure out that the last tip was a fake."

"If she has, I haven't heard anything about it," answered Red. "All I've gotten is an earful over all those blasted bushes."

Perkins picked up his coffee cup off the desk and took a thoughtful sip. "How about computers? Could we trick her into doing some computer research and tie her up that way for a while?"

Red hooted. "Perfect! All she really knows how to use is the word processing stuff and email anyway. The Internet to her is the Great Satan. I've got it—let me pretend to be talking on my phone to you. I have to run by her house anyway and take her to the store. Just give me 20 or 25 minutes and then give me a call. I'll mention something about loading the suspects into the search engine. It'll take a whole day for her to figure that out, then another one to actually do it. And she can do all her investigating in the safety of her own home and without terrorizing the community."

Myrtle had already made an interesting discovery over the newspaper that morning. Josh's article on Kitty's murder was as well-written as usual—what you'd expect from a person who'd been on the staff of the *New York Times*. But this time she noticed something different. The story not only made her feel like she was part of it, but it also made it sound as if *he* had been there when he'd interviewed Erma Sherman. And Myrtle knew it had been a phone interview. But all the facial descriptions had been included, and little things like, "She tugged nervously at her blouse collar."

Well. Josh probably hadn't been worried that Erma would take him up on his literary license, since she had such a crush on him. She was likely so flattered by the attention that she didn't even notice he'd added some details he couldn't possibly have known about. But it made her wonder. Had Josh embellished a story before and Parke's watchful eye had caught it? She hadn't had much time to dwell on this interesting idea because twenty minutes later, Red was driving her to the grocery store and grinning over her angry lecture about the need to respect mothers and not tinker with their cell phones when his own phone rang on cue. "What's that? Need me to check something online? Okay. Sounds like a lead...I'll check them out online. Yep, I'll load 'em into the search engine."

Myrtle busily scrabbled around in her cavernous pocketbook, as if searching for an elusive coupon or shopping list, while keeping her ears open. It irritated her that Red thought she was so clueless about computers that he could safely discuss them in front of her.

As Red and Myrtle arrived at the grocery store, both felt smug. Red was positive he'd created a time-consuming red herring to perplex his mother for hours (and in the knowledge that she'd forgotten to ask him to reprogram her cell phone) and Myrtle was smug in the knowledge that she'd searched people online before. She wasn't sure which suspect she was supposed to be checking into, but it didn't matter because it would take only minutes to check on each of them. She finished her grocery shopping in record time, throwing things into the shopping buggy and heading toward the check-out lanes. Red was amused as he loaded her bags into the back of his police car. His mother was dying to get back home and figure out what he'd been talking about. He felt sure that it was going to be a long project for her.

Red brought the grocery bags into Myrtle's house, her screen door slamming shut behind him. Setting the bags on the kitchen counter, Red asked, "Want me to help you put these things away, Mama?"

She shooed him off. "No, that's fine. I've got some things I need to do for Women of the Church, so you'd better get going. I can't think with you opening and shutting cabinet doors all the time." She watched as her smirking son walked out. Then she tossed a few things in the freezer and fridge and settled down in front of her computer. She'd *told* Red about the computer course she'd taken at the library a couple of years ago. Obviously, he hadn't been listening to her at the time.

Myrtle opened the search engine and stared thoughtfully at the screen. Who should she start with? She decided to go with Tippy and Benton. She typed in Benton's name first and saw more than ten entries. She was excited until further reading uncovered that all of the entries covered his political bid, town hall meeting transcripts, or Benton's civic involvement in various groups.

The search on Tippy was even more disappointing. There were half as many results and they all dealt with garden club and church involvement. Myrtle leaned back in her chair and looked at the computer screen glumly. What had she expected, though? She'd known both Benton and Tippy since they were babies. The only shocking news she'd come across was Benton's affair, and that was fairly predictable in this day and age.

She decided to check out a name she knew less about and searched Parke Stockard. Unfortunately, over 13,000 results came up on the screen. Myrtle sighed. Apparently, it was a pretty common name. She rummaged around in her recycling box until she came up with the *Bradley Bugle* that had Parke's obituary and full name. When she put in "Parke Frances Stockard," she got only fifty results—and all on the right Parke.

She grimaced. They were all old society column pieces that Parke had written for the *New York Post*. Parke's style of writing was the same as her *Lovely Living with Parke* column for the *Bradley Bugle*: lots of syrupy prose and a coy cozying up to the wealthy and well known. Myrtle supposed that Parke was the perfect person for the job. There was a small picture of Parke at a different event at the beginning of each column. She was inevitably perfectly groomed, gorgeous, and wearing something fabulous at an elaborate party with other well-heeled people. She read through as many celebrity sightings and descriptions of party attire as she could before giving up in disgust.

Idly, she looked up Althea Hayes and found some genealogical reference that Myrtle was already aware of, since Myrtle knew most family connections in the town of Bradley. There was also an old file regarding a Garden club benefit luncheon with Althea's name mentioned. Myrtle searched for Tanner and found very little. There was a website for the insurance company that Tanner had been employed with and it had a picture of all the (then) employees for the company. Tanner had a mildly distrustful look on his frog-like features as if he wasn't used to having his picture taken.

A search for Kitty Kirk brought up a story about her son being arrested for drug charges. A later, follow-up article mentioned her son going off to reform school.

Myrtle put in Cecil Stockard's name and weeded out the results that came back about university professors, Scuba divers, and actors until she had a page of results that dealt specifically with the Bradley Cecil. He had his own website that seemed to be a place where he bragged about the parties he'd gone to and the amount of alcohol he'd consumed. Friends of his posted their own pictures of themselves and the parties, and the friends looked like a rough-looking bunch. There was also a mug shot from an arrest several years earlier in New York for drug possession. "Well, he's been busy," Myrtle muttered. None of the information she pulled up really surprised her, though, or seemed to be connected to his mother's murder.

Finally, she plugged in Josh Tucker's name. Several pages of search results appeared, which got Myrtle very excited until she saw that most of the first page of results were all about the journalism prize he had won. Myrtle made a face. Wonder Boy. She had no idea what Red was looking for on the suspects, but it certainly wasn't leaping off the page. Although she still had a niggling feeling that she was overlooking something important.

Myrtle shut down her computer and looked thoughtfully at the dark screen. She knew Cecil was out of the picture, for the second murder anyway. Tippy wasn't very convincing at the church meeting; she was still in the running as a possible murderer, but she was onto Myrtle now and was going to clam up as soon as she saw Myrtle. She decided Althea was due another visit. Myrtle just couldn't shake the feeling that she knew something.

Myrtle would also have to endure another meeting with Wonder Boy. Josh might have some more information on the case and was still a suspect. Benton Chambers was another person she wanted to catch up with. There was just something about Benton that she didn't trust. He was spending a lot of his free time lying about where he was. It wouldn't take much of a stretch to cover up something as big as murder. She picked up her cane and purse to walk to town hall.

The town hall was located in the same building as the police department. Myrtle looked cautiously around her before turning the brass knob to go into the building. She didn't need Red to give her another lecture about detective work. She carefully made her way up the threadbare stairs to the main office.

Sitting at the old-fashioned wooden reception desk was a middle-aged woman flipping through a catalog. She looked up with some surprise when the door opened.

"Hi Lisa," said Myrtle. "Is Benton in?"

Lisa squinted at Myrtle over her bifocals. "Whatcha need Benton for?"

Small towns.

"Is he in? It's town business."

"I'll see if he's available to speak with you," answered Lisa imperiously. She whipped up the receiver of a 1980s era brown plastic desk phone with more buttons than the office had extensions. She pushed one of the extension buttons and cupped her hand over her mouth as she talked to Benton Chambers.

Lisa moved the receiver away from her and asked Myrtle, "What is this visit in reference to?" She didn't bother to hide her pleasure in making Myrtle spell it out after all.

"I'm having garbage collection problems," said Myrtle. Lisa reported to Benton, then set the phone carefully back on the hook, sniffed, and said, "He'll see you now." She picked up her catalog again, losing interest in Myrtle's unexpected appearance in the office.

Myrtle walked down a short hallway, turning on the little tape recorder in her pocketbook so she could review her conversation with Benton later. She pushed open an old, wooden door with "Benton Chambers" on a sign beside it. Tippy had obviously had a hand in decorating Benton's office. The town of Bradley sure couldn't afford Orientals on the floor or soft leather club chairs. A town that didn't replace ratty carpeting on the stairs sure didn't invest in oil paintings depicting fox hunts.

Benton was on the other side of a big desk and half-rose to his feet when Myrtle came in. "Miss Myrtle. You have a problem with your garbage collection? What can I do for you?" His politician face was on, although his smile was lost somewhere in his puffy jowls.

"Ah...yes. The truck used to come at 8:00 and now it comes at 7:00. I have to try to beat the truck every Tuesday and it's—exhausting."

Benton paused to puff a few times on his cigar. "Why not just set out your dumpster the evening before, Miss Myrtle? That way you don't have to rush around in the morning."

Myrtle beamed at him as if he were a star pupil. "What a wonderful idea, Benton! Yes, that's just what I'll do. I'll roll out the bin Monday night." She shook her head admiringly. "You certainly do have your thinking cap on. I'm just addled. This business with Kitty Kirk has completely scrambled my brain."

Benton shifted in his chair and hurried on, "Yes, well, you just prepare the night before and your garbage problems will be a thing of the past."

"Aren't you just broken up about Kitty? I can't believe that I was just going about my usual business while Kitty was being murdered. It just doesn't bear thinking about! What were *you* doing that day while poor Kitty was being killed?"

Benton frowned at her. "Miss Myrtle, that was a very demanding day. I spoke to the Women's Auxiliary in front of *many* ladies."

"All day?" asked Myrtle innocently.

"No, of course not. But I was all over town that day, running errands, speaking to groups, etc." He looked pointedly at his watch.

"Did you see many people while you were out all day?" Myrtle decided to drop all pretenses. If he really *were* all over town that day, then maybe he could give her some information about the other suspects.

Benton said, "Miss Myrtle, I hope you're not trying to do Red's job for him. I *can* tell you, although I hope you're not asking, that Tippy and I certainly had nothing to do with these murders. Period. And I did see some folks out that day—I saw Althea Hayes and her nephew Josh at Bo's Diner at lunchtime. And I saw Josh again later in the afternoon." He took a long drag at his cigar, then placed it on an ashtray. "I understand he had his own ax to grind with Parke Stockard over print space at the paper."

"It's interesting that you would know anything about that," said Myrtle.

Benton raised his eyebrows in surprise. "You, of all people, should know how small towns operate, Miss Myrtle! Good Lord, I can just walk from here to my car and find out more dirt on people's private business than a private eye." He snorted a humorless laugh, then said, "Detective work can be very dangerous, Miss Myrtle. You're probably just digging up harmless gossip, but if not—I've got to warn you. Don't mess in this stuff. It's police business and you'll only end up getting hurt." He punched at the air with a swollen finger in warning.

Myrtle gave an involuntary shiver, remembering the psychic's words at Crazy Dan's. "You're right, Benton. Right that I'm only after some gossip. Not too much for us old ladies to do, you know."

Benton seemed to relax. "That might be, Miss Myrtle. But there's always Bingo, you know. They play for rolls of stamps at the community center."

Myrtle nodded sadly and gathered up her pocketbook. "And good luck with your garbage collection," he called out as she closed the door behind her.

She was on her way out the door for what was going to be a fairly rigorous walk to Althea's when the phone rang.

Miles asked in his measured voice, "How are things going with the case?"

"Would you mind giving me a lift? I can tell you on the way. I'm trying to get over to Althea's and don't mind walking back, but roundtrip in this heat makes quite a workout."

A minute later they were in Miles' car and driving toward the Boulevard. Myrtle filled him in with the Internet search results and her failure to turn up any dirt. "So I decided to go harass Althea again. I'll squeeze some information out of her this time," she said in a determined voice.

"Want me to go in with you?" asked Miles.

"No, there's no point in putting her guard up any more than it is already. Besides," said Myrtle, batting her eyelashes outrageously, "she might end up becoming one of the lovesick members of the Miles Bradford Fan Club."

Miles frowned in irritation. "All right—I'll just drop you off then. When I get back home, how about if I double-check everything you pulled up online? Maybe I can find something you missed."

Myrtle nodded. "I do feel like there's something I should have noticed there—some clue I should have picked up on."

"And it's strange that Red would specifically mention checking out these folks if there wasn't anything to be found."

Miles pulled up into Althea's crepe-myrtle-lined driveway, braked, and turned off the engine. Myrtle sat quietly for a moment. "I've got it," she said, wagging her finger at Miles.

"I never caught on to it before, but both Josh Tucker and Parke Stockard moved here from New York City in the past couple of years. I wonder if they knew each other there."

Miles raised his eyebrows. "That's hardly likely, is it? You're talking about a city with eight million people in it."

"True. But they were both journalists."

"If a society columnist *is* a journalist," said Miles.

"So they could have known each other before moving to Bradley."

Miles squinted doubtfully. "They wouldn't have been running around in the same circles, surely? From all accounts, Parke was this glamorous beauty and Josh..."

"Was nobody's pretty child. I know. But journalists frequently get thrown together for work. I'll call Cecil." She glanced at her watch. "If he's awake."

"Awake? It's 1:00 in the afternoon!"

"He's something of a late-riser."

Cecil answered the phone after almost ten rings. "Hello?" he said in an annoyed voice.

"Cecil? It's Myrtle Clover. I know you're busy," Miles rolled his eyes and Myrtle bit back a laugh, "so I'll make it quick. I was just wondering if your mom knew Josh Tucker back in New York."

Now Cecil's voice had that snidely amused tone. "Doing some more nosing around, Miss Myrtle? Sure, they knew each other there. He covered lots of political candidates who went to the same parties that Mother wrote about for her column. I don't know anything more than that—I was in and out of rehab the last year we were there," he added sardonically.

"Do you think Josh Tucker might have wanted to kill your mother for some reason?"

"Nothing that I know about. But half the town wanted to murder Mother." He paused. "There was one thing. He blamed Mother for his uncle's heart attack—he really let me have it one day."

"Thanks, Cecil," said Myrtle. "You've been very helpful," she added in a surprised voice.

Myrtle opened the car door. "Thanks for the ride. Looks like they did know each other. I'll ask Althea a little more about her nephew."

Miles squinted at Althea's yard behind his wire-rimmed glasses. "I wouldn't have placed Althea at this particular house. It's got a kind of *Great Expectations* look about it."

Myrtle hadn't even taken a look at the yard, she was so wrapped up thinking about Cecil. "Good Lord. It does have that Satis House look of decomposing gentility, doesn't it?"

"Maybe Althea hired your yard man. That would explain a lot."

"Funny, Miles. No, not even Dusty would let a yard go this long. It would be too much work for him to cut the grass if he let it get this tall. Maybe Althea will mention something about it." Myrtle shut the passenger door firmly and waved to Miles with her cane as he drove away.

Althea's yard, usually a show-stopper, was wildly overgrown. The grass was long, the flower beds full of weeds. At least, Myrtle guessed they were weeds. They *were* flowering, but didn't look like the usual English garden weedy look that Althea went for. Japanese beetles invaded the trees. Myrtle frowned. This was not the usual gardening technique for a former president of the Bradley Garden club. Either Althea had let the yard man go, or else Tanner was the gardener-in-chief and nothing was really getting done without him. The yard had looked pretty bad when they'd visited before, but Myrtle had just figured Althea hadn't gotten around to doing it yet. Now she wondered if it was on Althea's to-do list at all.

Myrtle rang the doorbell and prayed fervently that Bambi wouldn't plow the door down and gobble her up with one gulp. A couple of minutes went by and Althea hadn't answered the door. Myrtle frowned again and looked over in the driveway. Althea's Cadillac was parked right there. Myrtle took an involuntary step backwards when Althea opened the door.

Chapter Seventeen

At first Myrtle didn't believe her eyes that the witchlike apparition that greeted her was the normally trim and elegant Althea. The hair that had always been neatly wound into a French twist lay in disarray on her shoulders in clumps. Bambi sat forlornly next to her, looking at his mistress with anxious eyes. Myrtle reached forward and held Althea by the arm. "What has happened, Althea? Something awful?"

She soon realized that something awful *had* happened.

Althea said vaguely. "I'm sorry I took so long. I couldn't find the door." She was dressed in a heavy flannel nightgown and thick robe and looked flushed.

Myrtle had the sudden sinking sensation that she knew the secret Althea desperately tried to hide over the past couple of weeks. She was in the early stages of Alzheimer's disease. Myrtle wasn't sure why she didn't notice it earlier—the way she mysteriously showed up in the sanctuary on the day of Parke Stockard's murder when she was supposed to be in the dining hall. The inappropriate clothes she wore to the book club meeting. The way she was avoiding the activities and people she usually enjoyed, to conceal her condition. The overgrown state of her beloved yard. The minister must know—that was why Nathaniel had so quickly changed the subject when Althea had materialized in the sanctuary. And now here was Althea on what was obviously a bad day for her—getting lost in her own home, apparently just waking up at 1:00 p.m., and wearing dirty clothing for the wrong season. Myrtle felt a wave of sadness come over her.

But Althea was leading Myrtle into the house. Myrtle wasn't entirely sure that Althea knew who she was, but she seemed determined to get Myrtle inside. "I'm glad you came to help," she was saying. "I can't find the iron anywhere."

Myrtle put out a hand and stopped Althea. "But I'm not here to help with that, Althea. It's Myrtle. I was coming over to talk with you about Parke Stockard's murder."

Althea knitted her brows together, a hint of awareness crossing her features. "Parke Stockard." She made a face. Yes, she remembered, all right. "That woman!"

She seemed deep in thought and Myrtle worried she might not be able to return from the fog. But Althea continued, "She was so awful to him. So ugly for a pretty woman. She ruined his life." She put her finger in front of her mouth. "But we don't need to tell anyone."

Myrtle felt as confused as Althea. "She ruined Tanner's life? By trying to get him to sell your property to her?"

Althea looked at Myrtle with blank eyes. "Tanner? No. She ruined *Josh's* life. My nephew, Josh Tucker."

Myrtle heard a buzzing in her ears while her brain whirled, processing the information. "She ruined *Josh's* life?"

Althea looked a little vague. "Said he didn't really talk to the people he wrote about in his articles. He got fired from his job. His wife divorced him and he had to come back home."

"But why was this such a big secret? And how do *you* know about it?"

"His parents were so proud of him. He didn't want them to know. And I knew—" She thought hard for a moment. "What were we talking about?"

Myrtle said, "How did you know about Parke getting Josh fired from his job?"

"Because I always took the *New York Times.* I was that proud of him. I read a story about him being suspended from the paper for problems with his stories." Althea looked sad, but then looked vacant again.

Myrtle mentally kicked herself for not making more out of the New York connection. She'd known they'd both spent time in New York and had recently moved to Bradley, but New York was such a big place, she hadn't seen a link. But with both of them working on newspapers in the same city? "Althea, I've got to go."

Althea nodded, still looking lost. The heavy nightgown and robe seemed to overwhelm her frail body, weighing her down. Myrtle looked around the once-neat and now very disorganized library and said sadly, "I'll call your daughter to get you some help."

Althea bobbed her head again. "Yes. That would be nice. I need some help." Myrtle left Althea walking in an aimless fashion towards the kitchen. Myrtle's head was still spinning from what she'd just learned. As she walked outside, her cell phone blared, "ARE YOU TRYING TO *KILL* ME?" She cursed, re-alizing she'd forgotten to ask Red to reprogram it back to a ring from a voice-tone. "*Sharper than a serpent's tooth*," Myrtle muttered.

It was Miles. "Listen, that search you did? Did you read all the results under Josh Tucker's name?"

Myrtle admitted, "Not nearly as well as I should have done, no. I stopped when I saw all that stuff about his award for the *Bugle*. I guess there's something about Josh being fired from the *Times*? Something to do with Parke Stockard?"

Miles sounded surprised. "Yes, actually. Oh, did you find that out from Althea?"

"I found out a lot at Althea's. More than I expected. But what exactly did you read online?"

"Apparently, the *Times* discovered that Josh Tucker had been fluffing up his articles with some fabricated details. Although it wasn't anything too major, the *Times* doesn't exactly specialize in fiction. They let him go, printed an apology to their readers, and mentioned Parke Stockard as the informant. Sounds like a motive for murder to me."

"Not only that, but Althea said that Josh's wife divorced him over the fallout from his being fired. So he ended up with no job and no wife. He came back home to Bradley, only to have Parke Stockard end up in the same place," said Myrtle.

"Seems like kind of a coincidence, doesn't it?" asked Miles.

"Not at all. If I remember correctly, either Cecilia or some-one mentioned that someone Parke knew kept talking about Bradley and what a great place it was. What do you want to bet that it was Josh or his ex-wife? Then Parke started looking for a warm climate and a hot real estate market and did a little checking on Bradley. When she found it was just what she was looking for, she moved down here," said Myrtle.

Miles said, "I'm going to try to do a little more checking on the computer. What are you doing? Do you need me to pick you up?"

"No, that's okay, Miles. I'm just going to run a quick errand." She wasn't ready to share with Miles what she knew and didn't want to tell him that she was going over to the *Bugle* to search for evidence in Josh's desk. A niggling voice in her head told her she should let her new sidekick in on her information. Luckily, Myrtle was good at ignoring little voices. She told herself that she'd spent too much time on this case to share the glory.

But that didn't mean she would be stupid. She needed to ensure that both Sloan and Josh Tucker were out of the office so she could search it. Luckily, as a columnist, she had a key to the newsroom. She dialed the number for the *Bradley Bugle*. Sloan answered. "Miss Myrtle. What can I help you with today?" Sloan's voice told her he wasn't exactly happy to hear her voice.

"Look, I need to come right over there. Right now. I—really need to talk to you about my column. You know how much everyone loves it and I think we need to expand it. Wonder Boy's articles are just so trite. Can't you cut them down a bit to make some room? I'll be right over there to talk to you about it."

Now Sloan sounded alarmed. "Okay. Right, Miss M. I'll be sure to be here."

Myrtle smiled. She could tell by his voice she'd succeeded in running him off. She'd get there and there'd be a note on the door saying that Sloan had to leave unexpectedly for an interview or something.

"Is Josh there, Sloan? There was something I needed to tell him, too."

Sloan handed off the phone in a hurry, eager to get off the line with the militant Myrtle.

"Josh? Hi, it's Myrtle. Listen, I overheard Red talking the other day and I have a lead for you on Kitty Kirk's murder. Yes, that's right. You need to go way out, though—-remember that house covered with hubcaps out the old highway—Crazy Dan's place? Yes, he apparently has some information. You're welcome, Josh."

Sloan gathered his things together while Josh hung up the newsroom phone. "I've got to get out of here. Myrtle Clover is coming over and she's on the warpath about her column again. Tell her anything—tell her I had an unexpected interview I had to do."

Josh stood up from his desk, his stooped shoulders looking even more hunched than usual. "She said she needed to talk to you?"

"No, she said she *had* to talk to me. Which means I don't need to be here." He headed for the door. "I'm grabbing some lunch, but don't tell her that. Make some excuse. A good one!"

Myrtle's mind worked hard on the new information and the walk to downtown seemed to go quickly. After an internal argument with herself, she decided it was time to share her findings with the police. With any luck, she'd find the evidence they needed in the next few minutes to add to her deductions. She dialed Red's number and got his voice mail. "Red? I've got some information about the case that you'll be interested in. Give me a call back when you have a minute."

As she walked towards downtown, the air seemed charged with electricity—and then actually *was* charged with electricity and a quickly corresponding *boom*! Myrtle glanced up at the sky, livid with billowing black clouds. She tottered down the street a little faster. These pop-up summer storms struck out of nowhere on these scorching hot days.

Myrtle slipped her key into the keyhole, pulled on the brass doorknob on the *Bradley Bugle*'s door, and walked into the paper-congested newsroom, standing in front of Sloan's desk.

It was empty. At least, it was empty of Sloan, not of stacks of paper, photographs, books, and the giant trophy. Myrtle smiled. She'd figured she'd run him off with her demand to talk to him about her column. She walked over to Josh's desk, which was covered with neat piles of folders and papers. Not sure what she was looking for, Myrtle opened the top drawer of his desk. If she could only find some evidence to match Josh with the murder scene. A deep voice behind her said, "Miss Myrtle? Dropping off a column?"

Chapter Eighteen

F ear knotted inside her, the color draining from her face as she slowly turned around. Josh stood close behind her, hooded gray eyes revealing nothing. He smiled, but it was a cold smile. He looked pointedly at her bare hands that weren't holding a column.

"It was kind of odd for you to call me with a lead, Miss Myrtle. Especially since you've been bound and determined to solve this case yourself. I thought I might just stick around and see what exactly you were up to."

Myrtle stood straight and faced him squarely, one hand leaning back on Sloan's desk, holding on to the corner for support. "No, Josh. I was looking for you, actually. I wanted to talk to you about Parke Stockard."

Remembering her tape recorder, she slipped her hand inside her dangling handbag to hit the record button. If nothing else, their recorded meeting would give all the evidence Red and Lieutenant Perkins needed for a day in court. Off balance, Myrtle dropped her cane.

Josh leaned over to pick it up, then swung it at her purse, sending it and all its contents flying across the floor. "Remember our lunch at Bo's Diner, Miss Myrtle? You seemed very proud to show off your reporting tools to me." He gave a mirthless laugh and kicked the contents of her purse a few feet away from them on the tile floor as he dropped the cane with a clatter to the floor.

Myrtle's voice came out like a croak. She cleared her throat and said, "I used to think that you blushed when you heard Parke's name because you were lovesick," said Myrtle. "But it wasn't a blush, was it? You were flushing with anger. You hated Parke Stockard for what she'd done to you."

Josh gave a dry laugh. "You've really been doing some investigating, haven't you? You must have finally caught up with Aunt Althea. I should have known she would end up giving it away."

"That Parke was the person who told the *Times* that you were fabricating details in your articles?"

Josh looked irritated. "That's just it. They were minor *details*. Small embellishments to make a couple of stories more interesting."

"You and Parke were friends in New York, then? She knew your articles weren't completely factual?" asked Myrtle.

Josh grunted. "Saying we were friends is a stretch. We were professional acquaintances who sometimes ended up in the same places. My ex-wife was a friend of hers, though."

"And one day you added some parts to a story that Parke knew weren't true," said Myrtle.

"It wasn't even a major story. It was just a piece about changes taking place in hospitals around the country. I was under deadline pressure and included some quotes to support the facts I already knew. Parke happened to be at a hospital benefit the following day and realized I couldn't have spoken to the people I quoted." Josh glowered. "She was always looking for information on people. Always looking for something to hold over their heads. A little bit of power to make them nervous with."

"So she told the paper. And they let you go."

Josh nodded. "They'd already had enough bad publicity with other journalists who printed inaccuracies. They fired me and printed a small article about the incident as quietly as possible. Not quietly enough for my wife to ignore, though. She left me. And not quietly enough for me to be able to get a job with any major newspapers in New York or elsewhere."

"So you came back home," Myrtle said. "And you got a job with the local paper and said you'd come back to take care of your parents. And you protected them from knowing what had happened in New York. In their mind, you came home to watch out for your aging parents and your wife was probably painted as no-good. Everything was fine for a while. Until Parke Stockard moved here."

Josh said nothing and Myrtle continued, "Parke probably wanted to be a big fish in a little pond. She was looking for a place with good real estate to be exploited. She remembered all the great things you said about Bradley. And maybe your ex-wife echoed those same things. Parke decided to move down here. You must have been horrified. She wasn't the kind to be discreet. But she was, perhaps, the type to blackmail other people."

Myrtle cocked her head to the side, wispy hair flying around her from the breeze off Sloan's oscillating fan behind her. "What happened that morning, Josh? Did she arrange to meet you at the church that morning since you were both already planning to be there? Did she threaten to tell everyone the truth about your past? And so you murdered her?"

Josh sighed, as if he couldn't believe he was having to go through so much trouble. "Actually, Miss Myrtle, it didn't happen that way at all."

Myrtle interrupted him. "No, I suppose it didn't. She would have threatened you *before* you went over to the church that morning. When you entered the sanctuary, you saw Parke Stockard on the floor—unconscious. You probably couldn't believe your good luck, could you? You thought she was dead and that someone else had done the favor for you. But then she stirred and you realized she was still alive. So you took the nearest thing to hand, the collection plate, and bashed her over the head with it. This time you knew she was dead.

"But Kitty Kirk saw something that she couldn't figure out. She saw you sneezing and your eyes running like you were still in the grip of an allergic reaction. She was very familiar with your allergy since she made sure every week that roses *weren't* part of the altar bouquet. When she said there weren't any roses, she meant that there weren't any roses on the grounds *outside* the church that would have made you sneeze like that. You'd been around the massive arrangement that Parke brought in."

Josh gave a forced laugh and wiped a trickle of sweat off his high forehead. "Miss Myrtle, that's the biggest crock I've ever heard. You're wasted on the helpful hints column—you should write novels."

"But you needed some security. You saw Kitty's face at the church that day and you knew she'd figure out what had happened eventually. At Parke's funeral, you made a special effort to swipe Cecil's checkbook. Even then you were looking ahead to the day when you might have to kill Kitty Kirk and pin the crime on Cecil Stockard."

Josh started to shake his head, but gave up the pretense. "You're pretty smart, aren't you, Miss Myrtle? Up until now. What made you think it was a good idea to come here and confront me?" He looked genuinely sorrowful. "I don't want to have to do this." Icy fear twisted inside her as he put his hand into his pocket and pulled out a knife.

Her stomach churned. "No," she said, after clearing her dry throat. "You just planned on having me drown. That night at the lake." Myrtle backed up into Sloan's desk and reached behind her with one hand. There had to be something on that crowded desk to use as a weapon.

Josh laughed. "Well, you'd just told me you had some information you needed to talk to me about. I knew how much you'd been snooping. What was I supposed to do?" he asked, as if his actions were perfectly reasonable.

He took the knife out of its sheath very calmly. "Actually, I didn't originally plan on drowning you. Smothering you made a lot more sense and would have been a lot easier, too. I know how all the old folks in Bradley keep their doors unlocked and windows open. I figured I'd just go in that night, hold a pillow over your face while you were sleeping." He shrugged. "Another old lady dies peacefully in her sleep."

Myrtle's heart pounded so hard she could feel it up in her head, throbbing. "Too bad I'm an insomniac. I didn't make it easy for you." Josh advanced towards her and frantically now, she fumbled behind her. Josh lifted up his arm and...

"ARE YOU TRYING TO KILL ME?" boomed the strident voice-tone behind them. Josh whirled around with the knife at the sound of Red's voice. Myrtle crouched down and grabbed her cane off the floor, then swung it with as much force as she could muster at Josh's knees.

Josh crashed down to the floor as Myrtle struggled up, pulling at Sloan's desk in her effort. With both hands she shoved the heavy, granite-based trophy off the desk and onto Josh's body, where it hit with a thud.

"Yoo-hoooo!" screeched a familiar voice and Myrtle could have wept with joy as the nasal sound of Erma Sherman reached her ears. Erma scolded, "You're not canoodling with my beau, are you—?" She cut herself off with a shriek at the sight of Josh with the knife lying on the floor beside him and Myrtle's white face. "You? You're the killer?" she asked the prostrate Josh. "The one *I liked*?"

"You harpy!" hissed Josh with weak anger. But Erma, pride affronted at having chosen a suitor so poorly, jabbed angrily at him with her umbrella.

Which was when Sloan Jones peeked in to see if Myrtle was still there or if it were safe to retrieve his forgotten wallet. His eyes flickered from the sight of Erma Sherman batting his award-winning reporter with an umbrella, to the large knife lying on the floor of his newsroom, to the pasty-faced and shaking octogenarian sinking into his swivel chair, and finally rested in dismay on the worst of the horrors—his adored trophy lying in pieces on the floor, its ornate quill pen top separated from the granite base. "My trophy!"

"ARE YOU TRYING TO KILL ME?" blared again behind them and Myrtle scooted over with the rolling desk chair to scoop the phone off the floor and answer it. "Red?" she asked weakly.

An hour later, Myrtle was home again with her feet up and a glass of wine in her hand. Red stood in front of her, alternating between relief she was all right and extreme exasperation. Lieutenant Perkins sat calmly, looking slightly out of place on her floral sofa, waiting for Myrtle to swallow the big gulp from her glass and continue her story. Red was less patient. "You know you're lucky you didn't kill him, Mama. He's in the hospital for concussion. You punched his lights out."

"He didn't deserve it?" asked Myrtle imperiously.

At a loss for words, Red just opened his mouth and closed it again.

Perkins jumped in. "So I understand, Mrs. Clover, how you figured out that Josh Tucker murdered Parke Stockard. You picked up on the New York connection and figured out Kitty Kirk's comment about the roses. Did you just assume, then, that he'd also killed Mrs. Kirk?"

Myrtle shook her head. "What actually clued me in was that at Parke's funeral, Josh came back into the church to find something he said he'd lost. I was more aggravated with him than anything else at that point because he was sneezing like crazy from all the roses in the sanctuary and I was trying to listen in on Cecil and Cecilia's argument."

Red gave a gusty sigh, which Myrtle ignored.

"I was so focused on trying to listen in at the time that I really wasn't paying attention to what he was doing. He, of course, was picking up the checkbook to incriminate Cecil later on."

Perkins frowned. "Was he even sitting that far up in the sanctuary originally?"

"Oh, he was taking a risk. But he had been sitting in one of the first few pews. I guess he just reached over to the front row and took it."

Perkins said, "So he knew even then that he was going to kill Kitty Kirk?" His voice sounded skeptical.

"No, he was just getting the checkbook for insurance. He'd seen Kitty's expression when he was sneezing outside the church the day Parke was killed. But Kitty was still thinking that *she* had killed Parke. She'd hit her upside the head pretty hard and left before checking to see if Parke was still alive."

Red piped in, "And I guess you were on his hit list, too, Mama. That night you ended up in the lake."

"I don't know," said Myrtle thoughtfully. "He might have just been trying to warn me. I'd told him earlier that I had something important I wanted to tell him." When Red rolled his eyes, she retorted, "Well, I wanted to talk to him and pick his brain to find out what he knew! He's a reporter, after all."

"A reporter who likes making up stories," said Red.

"I don't think that was an all-the-time thing. He probably used it when he was coming up on a deadline and needed some embellishment. But he chose to do it around the wrong person. Parke liked holding information over people's heads."

Perkins closed his notebook. "I have to hand it to you, Mrs. Clover. You did a great job solving this case."

Red snorted. "Oh, come on. None of that stuff would have held up in court, you know."

"Which is why I had to search for some evidence to connect him to the crimes! Except Josh wasn't supposed to be there."

"Well," said Perkins soothingly. "It's lucky for us that you thought this through. You've taken a very dangerous and desperate person off the streets."

Myrtle sipped her wine. "Funny how it ended up. I thought for the longest time that the murderer was Benton Chambers. I'd gotten the information from Crazy Dan about Benton's affair," she admitted, stealing a sideways glance at Perkins. He and Red exchanged a startled look. Probably wondering where she'd gotten that lead, she guessed.

"So what's your next move, Mama. Plan on becoming part of the space program? Marine biologist? Any other hats you feel like wearing?"

Myrtle smiled at the admiration in Red's voice.

"Oh, I think I'll take a break for a while and let the world try to save itself. Just sit back, watch my soaps. Maybe Miles and I can start our own book club. There's a need for serious literary discussion in the town of Bradley."

Red looked relieved. Myrtle winked at Perkins. Perkins didn't feel relieved at all.

Perkins stood up and walked over to open Myrtle's front door. "Interesting gnome display, Mrs. Clover. I wouldn't have pegged you for a collector."

"Yes," said Myrtle brightly. "I'm full of surprises. I think I'm ready to put them away for a while, though. Red looked at her with surprise and she said, "Considering how well Altar Guild duty turned out," she added under her breath to Red as Perkins walked out.

Red gave a contented sigh. "Everything's back to normal. Jean-Marc is going back to France in a week and there are no crazed murderers running around. The gnomes will be hibernating in the shed. Life is good." Red walked towards the door, then turned and said, "By the way, Mama, Sloan Jones said to give him a call about your writing a front-page story on the capture of Josh Tucker."

Myrtle sniffed. "Sure, he wants my help now that Parke is dead and his star reporter is in jail."

"It's the least you can do, Mama, considering you smashed his big trophy."

"Well, it wasn't exactly the prettiest trophy I'd ever laid eyes on. Who would think to make a huge quill pen into a trophy?"

Red said, "That ugly trophy saved your life, Mama. You're lucky you had a convenient instrument to brain him with."

"I guess it just proves the old saying right, Red: the pen really is mightier than the sword."

About the Author:

Elizabeth writes the Southern Quilting mysteries and Memphis Barbeque mysteries for Penguin Random House and the Myrtle Clover series for Midnight Ink and independently. She blogs at ElizabethSpannCraig.com/blog, named by Writer's Digest as one of the 101 Best Websites for Writers. Elizabeth makes her home in Matthews, North Carolina, with her husband. She's the mother of two.

Sign up for Elizabeth's free newsletter to stay updated on releases:

https://bit.ly/2xZUXqO

This and That

I love hearing from my readers. You can find me on Facebook as Elizabeth Spann Craig Author, on Twitter as elizabethscraig, on my website at elizabethspanncraig.com, and by email at elizabethspanncraig@gmail.com.

Thanks so much for reading my book...I appreciate it. If you enjoyed the story, would you please leave a short review on the site where you purchased it? Just a few words would be great. Not only do I feel encouraged reading them, but they also help other readers discover my books. Thank you!

Did you know my books are available in print and ebook formats? Most of the Myrtle Clover series is available in audio and some of the Southern Quilting mysteries are. Find the audiobooks here.

Please follow me on BookBub for my reading recommendations and release notifications.

I'd also like to thank some folks who helped me put this book together. Thanks to my cover designer, Karri Klawiter, for her awesome covers. Thanks to my editor, Judy Beatty for her help. Thanks to beta readers Amanda Arrieta and Dan Harris for all of their helpful suggestions and careful reading. Thanks to my ARC readers for helping to spread the word. Thanks, as always, to my family and readers.

Other Works by Elizabeth:

Myrtle Clover Series in Order (be sure to look for the Myrtle series in audio, ebook, and print):

Pretty is as Pretty Dies
Progressive Dinner Deadly
A Dyeing Shame
A Body in the Backyard
Death at a Drop-In
A Body at Book Club
Death Pays a Visit
A Body at Bunco
Murder on Opening Night
Cruising for Murder
Cooking is Murder
A Body in the Trunk
Cleaning is Murder
Edit to Death
Hushed Up
A Body in the Attic
Murder on the Ballot
Death of a Suitor (2021)

Southern Quilting Mysteries in Order:
Quilt or Innocence
Knot What it Seams
Quilt Trip
Shear Trouble
Tying the Knot
Patch of Trouble
Fall to Pieces
Rest in Pieces
On Pins and Needles
Fit to be Tied
Embroidering the Truth
Knot a Clue
Quilt-Ridden (2021)
The Village Library Mysteries in Order (Debuting 2019):
Checked Out
Overdue
Borrowed Time
Hush-Hush
Where There's a Will (2021)
Memphis Barbeque Mysteries in Order (Written as Riley Adams):
Delicious and Suspicious
Finger Lickin' Dead
Hickory Smoked Homicide
Rubbed Out
And a standalone "cozy zombie" novel: Race to Refuge, written as Liz Craig